THE AMISH DREAMER

BOOK 5 THE AMISH WOMEN OF PLEASANT VALLEY

SAMANTHA PRICE

AMISH ROMANCE

CHAPTER 1

NEWLY MARRIED JACOB and Rebecca had done their post-wedding visitation duty and they were heading home from the bus station in a taxi. For weeks, they'd visited the people who couldn't make it to the wedding and now Rebecca wanted nothing more than to settle into married life with Jacob and her new stepson.

"Are you happy to be an instant *mudder?*" Jacob asked with a grin as though he'd read her thoughts.

She looked at his smiling eyes and warm face. That look was something she'd never get too much of. "I am. 'Happy' isn't a good enough word." She tightened her grip on his hand. They always held hands when no one could see them. "And I'm looking forward to settling into a routine of sorts." Rebecca looked out the window at the farms they were passing, glad to be back in familiar surroundings. Being a midwife, she'd never have a regular daily routine like other young married women, but that was part of her calling.

Everything had worked out perfectly for her and she thanked God every day for her new family. With the constant demands of midwifery, she'd convinced herself she'd never marry, figuring she'd remain single like Marilyn, the midwife who'd trained her. Then Jacob had come along. When Jacob's wife had died, his sister, Anne, had come to live with him and now Anne was only too happy to stay on and look after Micah whenever Rebecca was out on a job. "I'm so glad to be back before Mary has her *boppli.* I told her to wait and she must've listened to me."

Jacob chuckled. "Most pregnant women I've known don't want to wait for anything or anyone."

"I guess that's true and I might find that out first-hand soon enough, for myself."

He took hold of her hand. "Very soon I hope. I can barely wait until Micah has a younger *bruder* or *schweschder* to play with."

She smiled at him and then she noticed the taxi was turning left instead of right. "We're going the wrong way."

"Nee, we're going the right way."

"Our place is back that way."

"Nee." He chuckled. "This is my surprise."

By the impish grin on his face, she knew their house was ready and they wouldn't be going back to their rental. "Are we in our new *haus* already?"

He smiled and nodded. "We sure are. I'm afraid we'll have a lot of unpacking to do. Or, I should say, you'll have a lot of unpacking to do because I have to start work tomorrow. Anne said she left most of it for you to manage because she didn't know where you wanted things."

"That was thoughtful." So far Anne hadn't stepped on her toes as the female head of the household, but Rebecca had only stayed one night in their rental house after their wedding before they left to visit people. "How does she like the *grossdaddi haus?*"

"She loves it. It's as big as a small *haus* and as comfortable as it can be."

"Good. She deserves that since she left everything to come live with you." Anne had left her old life and rushed to help Jacob when his wife had died a short time after Micah was born. Jacob had decided to stay on in Pleasant Valley where his wife had been raised and it wasn't long after that Rebecca and he had fallen in love.

"Don't get too excited when you see the *haus.* It still has some things that need doing, but it's ready enough."

"I can't wait to see it. I haven't even seen it with the walls up."

"I'll get Timothy out to finish the rest of the work soon."

Rebecca nodded at the suggestion. Her older brother was a builder and had been out of work the last she knew.

When they stepped out of the taxi, Anne hurried over to them and gave each of them a hug. "Micah's asleep," was the first thing she said to them.

"We've missed him so much," Jacob said.

"I think he's grown. He's going through another growth spurt."

"We'll see him as soon as we put our bags inside and after I give Rebecca a tour of the *haus*." Jacob took the two bags from the driver as they were pulled out of the trunk.

Anne was first to their front door and she pushed it open for them. *"Ach,* I'm sorry. You should show her around, Jacob."

Jacob gave an embarrassed chuckle.

"Why don't you both show me through?" Rebecca looked from brother to sister.

"You first," Anne said to Jacob.

Jacob went first and the two ladies followed.

"I can't get over the space, and the furniture is in here already. Who did all this work?" Rebecca asked.

"Timothy did some and other people helped out when he needed them."

"I didn't know where you wanted everything, Rebecca. I'll help you move it if you want to change it around," Anne said.

"It looks fine to me." Rebecca took another look around, suddenly feeling very grown up. She finally had her own household to run. "It feels like home."

When they reached the large kitchen, Anne opened

two of the cupboards. "I've unpacked a few basic necessities to get you started, but of course we can rearrange however you wish."

"*Denke.* I'll see to it all tomorrow when I come back from visiting my folks. And, I'll have to check on Mary to see how she's doing. I half expected to get a call while we were away to say that she'd had the *boppli* already."

"*Nee,* she hasn't and if she had, I would've heard." Anne shook her head.

After they were done looking around the house, they went into Anne's *grossdaddi haus* to fetch Micah.

"Oh, look. He's sleeping so soundly." Rebecca wished she could sleep so heavily, but with her job a deep sleep was a rare gift. She was always expecting her pager to sound or the phone to ring.

Jacob put a hand on his sister's shoulder, and whispered, "*Denke* for looking after him, Anne. We'll fetch him when he wakes."

"Okay, you two get settled, and you can take him home after you have the evening meal here with me. I prepared something for you."

Rebecca tried to smile. It had saved her work, but she would've preferred to have a romantic dinner alone with her new husband. Especially with this being the very first time they'd eat a meal in their new home. "Is that what smells so delicious?"

Anne nodded.

"*Denke.* I'll have to go to the markets tomorrow to fill the cupboards."

"I have some boxes of canned goods and jars of preserved fruits in your kitchen."

Now Rebecca felt bad for being a little resentful. Anne was so good for looking after Micah, and Rebecca knew she'd have to stop feeling that way. "*Denke,* Anne. I'll check what there is so I don't double up." It was going to be sort of like living with her *mudder*-in-law. She'd feel she had to be the best cook, have the cleanest *haus* and be careful to always make the most economical choices with the food shopping.

THE NEXT MORNING when Rebecca was ready to visit her mother, she knocked on Anne's door to collect Micah since he'd ended up staying there the night. Anne had made one excuse after another why he should stay with her. It was okay for now but Rebecca knew she'd have to monitor the situation. She wanted Micah close to her, so he could get used to her as his new mother.

Anne opened the door.

"Hello, Anne. I'm here to collect Micah. I'm taking him to visit my folks."

Anne's mouth twisted slightly. "That's not necessary. He can stay here with me instead of being jiggled about in the buggy. You can collect him when you get back. I've got his things packed ready for you."

"He won't be jiggled about. I'm not that bad a driver and he'll be secure in his seat. Besides, my *mudder* would like to see him."

Anne blinked rapidly. "She saw him at the meeting, Sunday last."

Rebecca didn't want to stand there arguing with Anne. "Would you like to come with us?"

"Nee, I'll stay here with little Micah."

"Are you sure that's okay? Wouldn't you like a break from looking after him now that I'm back?"

"Nee, it's perfectly fine. Come and see him before you go."

"Okay." Rebecca walked into the small kitchen where Micah was propped up in the high chair. He was now her son and she didn't like being "invited" to see him. She wanted to take him now she was back. "Hello, Micah," she whispered as she leaned down and kissed the top of his head and he smiled at her. "He's so cute."

"Jah, he is. I'll have him ready for you when you finish visiting your *mudder,* okay? You can see he's happy here and rested." Anne gave her a lovely bright smile and Rebecca knew her fears were unfounded.

"Okay I'll do that." She turned back to Micah. "I'll see you when I get back and I'll take you home to your new bedroom."

. . .

REBECCA HITCHED her buggy and traveled to her childhood home, a little sad to be going without her new stepson. Her younger brothers would be at school and her teenage brothers would be at work, but she was anxious to see her mother whom she'd missed dreadfully. When she pulled up outside her old home, her mother ran out to her. Rebecca jumped down from the buggy and they met with a hug.

"It's so good to see you back."

"It's good to be home." Being so much taller than her mother, she rested her arm comfortably around her mother's shoulder. "What's been going on?"

"You won't believe it." *Mamm* shook her head. "So much has happened. Come inside and I'll tell you all about it."

They walked into the house arm-in-arm. "I can't wait to hear everything."

"So much, so much. Sit down first. You'll need to be sitting when I tell you."

"Is it bad?"

"*Nee,* it's good. I'm certain."

Once they were inside, Rebecca hurried to sit down at the kitchen table. "Mary hasn't had the *boppli* yet, has she?"

Mamm picked up the teakettle. "*Nee,* but Timothy's getting married."

"What?" Rebecca shrieked. Her mother giggled and once she'd put the teakettle onto the stove she sat down around the corner from Rebecca, who was trying to get over the shock. "It's true?"

"I'm not fibbing."

Rebecca tried to think of who her older brother might be marrying and she couldn't think of anyone likely. "Not May?"

Her mother laughed. *"Nee.* Not May. Do you remember Abigail, a young woman visitor who was at your wedding?"

In her mind's eye, she mentally pictured all the visitors at her wedding. "Abigail? The one with the cute young *dochder?"*

"That's right."

Rebecca pulled a face. "Don't tell me he's going to marry her?"

"That's right," *Mamm* repeated.

Her mother seemed pleased about it, but Rebecca wasn't so certain. "This doesn't feel right. Don't you think it's a little rushed? They haven't known each other for long. You can't fall in love with someone in that short a space of time."

"Love is love. Who's to say how long it takes? It can be instant with a special feeling in your stomach." Her mother put her hand on her tummy.

"Well let's just hope that feeling in the stomach doesn't turn into nausea if things don't go as well as he hopes."

Her mother's lips drew together tightly. Was it disapproval Rebecca detected on her face? *Mamm* finally said, "That's funny coming from you with your own hasty marriage to Jacob."

"That was months. I knew him for months before we married. This is just days. Two weeks? Are you kidding me? Are you and *Dat* really condoning this potential catastrophe?" Rebecca couldn't see why her mother seemed happy about it. *Dat* would've agreed to things, too, as long as *Mamm* was happy.

The smile was gone from *Mamm's* face. "I thought you'd be happy for your *bruder.*"

"If she wasn't a stranger, I would be. If she was from this community I'd be happy, but she's not. We don't know her. It's a shock." Rebecca sighed and rubbed her forehead. "It's just odd to come back and hear he's getting married to someone I don't even know." She stared into her mother's eyes wondering how they could allow Timothy to marry a stranger. Not only that, there was a child to consider in all this. It was reckless and yet her father must've agreed to it since her mother looked so happy.

"I didn't think you'd have such a problem with it. I thought you'd be pleased."

"Where is he?" She had to talk some sense into Timothy.

"He's over at her *haus* working on it."

"Abigail has a *haus* already? She works quickly on all fronts."

"She bought it. Timothy was showing her all the places for sale and she bought one and is leasing it until all the final paperwork is done. Timothy is helping her figure out what to do with things. She was staying in your bedroom before that and that's how they got to know one another."

"My bedroom? I haven't even got my things out of it yet."

"That's all packed up and in the barn, ready for you to collect."

"Hmm, it seems like he couldn't wait to get me out. At my wedding, Timothy told me you said he could have my old room."

Mother nodded and her lips turned upward slightly at the corners. "I do remember there was a misunderstanding about that."

Rebecca sighed heavily. "I'll have Jacob come by later and pick up my things from the barn. I hope it was all packed carefully and not just tossed out there recklessly."

"Oh, Rebecca, you're so dramatic sometimes. Of course everything was well packaged up."

"I'll see for myself." Rebecca headed out to the barn while her mother stayed in the kitchen. Had she been there while Timothy was courting this woman, he would've asked her advice and she would've begged him to slow down. Obviously, no one had guided him in love and marriage.

Before Rebecca reached the barn, she noticed May heading up the driveway toward the house, driving her buggy. May's twin sister, April, had left the community after making up dreadful lies over Jacob. There really was no nastiness in May, Rebecca knew, except when her sister influenced her. She waited for the buggy to draw closer and May stopped the buggy close to the barn. "Hi, May."

"Rebecca! Someone said you were back." May stepped down and hurried to her. "It's so good to see you — I've come to you for advice, if that's okay."

"Sure." Anything to keep her from thinking of the mistake her brother was about to make. "What's on your mind?"

May inhaled deeply. "The thing is that I like someone and he's a widower and I know you've just married a widower, so I'm hoping you'll give me some insight."

Rebecca knew there were a couple of widowers in their large community, but she couldn't think of which one May would possibly like. "Who is he?"

"I don't want you to say anything."

"Of course I won't."

"It's William Bronstein."

Rebecca slowly nodded as she pictured William Bronstein. He was a handsome man with two daughters who weren't yet teenagers. "William is a nice man. What kind of advice are you looking for?" Just as May opened her mouth to respond, the phone in the barn rang. "Just a minute, sorry. I'll have to get that." Rebecca hurried to get to the phone before it stopped ringing. "Hello."

"Rebecca?" It was a man's voice and he sounded urgent.

"Samuel?"

"She's gone into labor. Hurry."

"I'll be right there." Because of his panicked voice, she didn't ask questions about how long Mary had been having contractions or whether she was in pain. Their house wasn't far, so she'd find out for herself. She turned around to face May, who'd followed her into the barn. "Do me a huge favor?"

"Yeah, what is it?"

"Go to my new *haus* and tell Anne that Mary is in labor and I don't know when I'll be back." Rebecca was glad she'd grabbed her bag of midwife necessities on her way out this morning, a habit Marilyn had ingrained in her from the earliest days of training.

"Sure."

"Do you know where my new place is?"

"The one that Timothy was working on?"

"Yeah."

"I know it, but I need your advice first."

Rebecca rushed past her. "I can't talk now. I must go to Mary."

May was hot on her heels. "When can we talk? Shall I come to you?"

Rebecca stopped still. "I'll come to you as soon as I can. Her *boppli's* coming and I must go. As soon as I get the next bit of time, which might be tomorrow or maybe the day after, I give you my word I'll come to you. We can sit down and have a big talk, okay?"

"Okay."

She leaned forward and gave May a quick hug. "Can you also tell my *mudder* where I'm going?"

"Sure."

Rebecca jumped into the buggy and headed to Samuel and Mary's house. Micah was the last baby born in that house. Things had gone well with the birth but things had gone downhill rapidly with the death of Jacob's wife soon afterwards. That was at the forefront of Rebecca's mind. The other thing was, she would have to watch what she said in front of everyone because no one apart from herself and Mary and Samuel knew that this was Mary's second birth, not her first.

CHAPTER 2

MAY WAS UPSET that Rebecca had no time for her. She'd always seen Rebecca as a friend. She walked over to the bishop's front door and knocked.

A surprised Hannah opened the door. "May." Then Hannah looked past her at Rebecca's buggy moving away rapidly. "Where's Rebecca going?"

"She had a call from Mary. She's in labor."

A smile chased away Hannah's frown. "That is good news. And they'll both be delighted Rebecca came back just in time. *Gott* is so *gut.*"

"I guess so. I mean, *jah,* He is."

"I just made tea. Will you join me?"

"Nee denke, I have to get home. I've heaps to do."

"Okay." Hannah leaned on the door post. "How's April?"

"She's doing okay."

"Do you hear from her much?"

"We write all the time. I get a letter from her every week."

"You must miss her."

"I do. Well, bye, Mrs. Shroder."

"Bye, May."

She turned away from Hannah thinking about whether she really missed April. If she searched her heart, she'd have to admit she did, but she certainly didn't miss the commotion that always surrounded April or how people judged her as being just like April. She was nothing like her sister and with April gone, she could be who she really was inside instead of being overshadowed by her older twin. Just because April was born a few minutes before she was did not give April permission to boss her around.

"Say hello to your parents for me," Hannah called after her.

"I will," she said with a half-hearted wave over her shoulder.

When Hannah closed the door, May dragged her feet the rest of the way to the buggy with her shoes making crackling sounds as she rolled them over the tiny pebbles. When she reached the horse, she took hold of the leather reins and climbed into the driver's seat. Convinced life was passing her by, she turned the horse and buggy to face the road. Her beloved horse, Nigel, moved forward without her needing to utter a word.

Why didn't life go the way she wanted it to, just like

Nigel did? Oftentimes all she had to do was think where she was going, left or right, and he'd head in that direction. She slumped lower in her seat. Soon everyone her age would be married and she'd be the only one left single. She'd had a small crush on Timothy and then Abigail had moved in with Timothy's family and that was the end of that, before anything ever got started.

It was an awful feeling to be left on the shelf like a piece of bad and unwanted mottled-looking fruit. If she could just get William Bronstien to notice her, things could be different. She knew she'd be a good mother to his two girls. They were young enough that she could teach them to sew and keep house just like her mother had showed her and April.

As her horse moved slowly back home, clip-clopping along the dirt-packed road, she dreamed of being married to William. His face would light up as he sat down to one of her delicious meals. Then, a few years along, their house would be filled with the laughter of young children. She would have many of them, so she'd always have a small baby to hold and to cuddle. So caught up was May in her beautiful daydream, she didn't notice another buggy until it was upon her. Jeff was in the driver's seat of the other buggy and he waved with his arm out the side of the buggy.

Her heart sank. If only William liked her even half as much as Jeff Whiley seemed to ... Jeff had made no secret of his feelings, and he wasn't a bad person. It was just that she didn't particularly like the way he looked. He was so boyish, with his freckled face and slender frame. Besides that, Jeff was only a shade taller than she, whereas William towered over her.

She was in no mood to talk to Jeff, but still, she fixed a smile on her face as he stopped in the center of the quiet backroad. She gave Nigel the signal to stop and he obeyed. "Hello, Jeff."

"May." He nodded at her. "What are you doing out this way?"

"I just called in to see Rebecca. She's back and was visiting her *mudder*. Then she had to rush away to deliver Mary's *boppli*."

He raised his eyebrows. "That is good news. Another member of the community." He chuckled. "If new people don't join us, we'll just breed 'em. Either way *Gott* gives us an increase to our population."

Squirming in her seat at his awful comment, she nearly told him how horrible it sounded. It was beyond her why he thought it funny. "People do join us, though. A family did last summer and then an *Englisch* man just three months ago."

"I was half joking."

"Many people do join us," she repeated.

Now he wasn't smiling. "I know they do. What are you doing with the rest of your day?"

"Helping my *mudder*. Aren't you working?"

"Not today. I've got the day completely free and

clear. I just stopped at your place and your *Mamm* said you might be out this way."

"Jeff Whiley, have you been following me?"

"Definitely not! I was looking for you."

May shook her head. "It's the same thing."

"Well, not really. To follow someone, you must see where they're going before they set out and stay right behind them."

She swiped her hand through the air to put an end to that topic. "Why did you want to see me?"

"I wanted to know if you'd want to hang out today."

She wrinkled her nose. "'Hang out?'"

"You know, do something together. Just you and me."

She shook her head. "I've got far too much to do helping *Mamm*."

Jeff stared back at her. "She said you were free today. I stopped in there just now."

Anger welled within her. How could her mother betray her like that? "She would say that because she doesn't realize all the things that have to be done today. There is far too much to do and I can't let her do it all alone. She's such a kindly woman, trying to let me off all the hard work."

"I didn't see there was much work. You can't have much with only you and your folks."

"There's the cleaning, cooking, raising the vegetables and keeping the garden tidy. My *vadder* hates an untidy garden. I'll get into terrible trouble and he'll go after me with the strap if the *haus* is messy when he comes home."

Jeff's eyes opened wide. "Is that so? Aren't you a little too old to get a belting?"

She didn't know if he believed her or not, but since it had slipped out of her mouth, she had to continue. Her father had taken the strap to her and April only once when they let all the horses out of the paddock when they were nine. They had been plenty old enough to know better. They got into big trouble that day and she never forgot it. "So, you see, I don't really have any free time. I'm sorry, Jeff."

"That's okay. Can I take you home from the singing on Sunday night, then?"

"Well, you could, except I'm not going to the singing this Sunday." She definitely wasn't now. Before he could ask about the Sunday after that, she said, "If you'll excuse me, Jeff. I'm very late. My *mudder's* expecting me. Goodbye." She flicked the reins lightly on her horse's rump and normally that would've been enough to have him walk or even take off at a trot, but he didn't move. "Come on, Nigel." She flicked the reins on his rump again. "Nigel, forward!" She used her best angry voice and when that didn't work, she clicked her tongue and then slapped the reins harder against his rump. He moved his head up and down and then took one step.

When Jeff laughed, she looked over at him about to say something rude when Nigel took off at a spritely pace. "Bye, Jeff," she called over her shoulder. Once she was well past him, she looked in her rearview mirror. Jeff was still staring at her even though his buggy was faced in the opposite direction. *"Denke* for nothing, Nigel. You really should've obeyed me back there. What came over you?" His ears were turned back slightly and when she finished speaking, his ears moved forward. "Stupid horse," she muttered under her breath.

Before she got home, she remembered Mary was in labor and she said a prayer for the health and safety of Mary and the baby.

CHAPTER 3

AT THREE THE FOLLOWING MORNING, Rebecca was pleased to hand Mary a perfectly healthy baby boy.

"Is he okay?" Mary moved her hands all over her son as he lay tummy-down on her chest.

"He's perfectly healthy. He's a good color, and he's breathing well and his heart and lungs sound perfect."

Samuel reached down and kissed Mary on her forehead. "We have a beautiful *boppli. Denke.*"

"It's a boy?" Mary asked.

"That's right," Samuel said softly.

Mary looked up at Samuel. "I know we already chose a name for a boy, but I want to change it. I'd love it if we called him after you."

He chuckled. "Won't that be confusing?"

"*Nee*, we'll call him Sam." She leaned down and kissed the baby's head.

"If that's what you want."

"*Jah.* Little *boppli* Sam. Do we need to cut the cord now, Rebecca? Or, is that done?"

"We still need to do that. There's no hurry. We can do that in a minute." Rebecca turned away to give husband and wife privacy with the newborn while she cleaned up the room.

Everything had gone perfectly, the same as it had at Mary's first birth with Lois.

As Rebecca cleaned the room, her mind was drawn back to the events of many years ago. Mary told Rebecca her first husband walked out on her when she was pregnant. She'd followed him hoping he'd change his mind and then with her own eyes she witnessed him run down by a truck.

Having had bad experiences in many foster homes herself, all Mary wanted for her child were two loving parents and a normal life. She chose to give her baby to her childless friend, Beth and her husband. No one would ever know the truth — Mary and Beth went away together in the later months of Mary's pregnancy and Beth had returned with 'her' baby, Lois. No one ever knew any different.

Then the fateful day came when Beth and her husband were killed in a tragic accident, but Lois was spared. Gone was Lois's stable life. Before Mary could confess that Lois was her child, Samuel had already stepped in to look after the child he thought was his niece. Mary volunteered to help out with Lois while Samuel worked, and instead he'd hired her as nurse-maid. From there, Mary and Samuel fell in love.

Mary had told Rebecca that Samuel found out about Lois's true identity before he and Mary were married. Mary didn't tell Rebecca details of exactly how Samuel had found out, but Rebecca was glad the secret between the couple hadn't continued.

The three people in that room were the only ones who knew of Lois's true identity. Samuel was not Lois's uncle, but he was now her stepfather. Mary wasn't Lois's stepmother, she was her real mother.

Rebecca was uncomfortable with Mary's decision to keep the ruse going and she'd told her so on more than one occasion. Were they going to tell Lois that Beth was her mother when she wasn't? What good would it do to tell Lois that her mother had died when her mother was right there with her? For some reason, Mary and Samuel were comfortable with their decision to leave things as they were.

One thing Rebecca knew was that Samuel and Mary would lose respect within the community for keeping that secret if the true story ever came out.

After a few minutes had passed, the cord was cut and clamped, and baby Sam was diapered and bundled into a soft wrap. There was no need to help Mary as she usually had to do with first-time mothers. Mary knew what to do and how to feed young Sam.

A couple of hours later, it was time for Rebecca to leave the couple with their precious gift from *Gott.* "I have my pager on me and do you know the phone number of my new *haus?*"

Samuel nodded. "I do. I know how to get hold of you."

"Call me any time, at any hour if you need to."

"Denke, Rebecca," Samuel said.

"You're very welcome." Rebecca looked down at the young baby. "This is what I love to do. I can't think of anything better." She blinked back the emotional tears that always threatened whenever she helped a new life come into the world.

REBECCA ARRIVED home just as the sun was peeping above the horizon and spreading its warm beams across the sky. It hadn't been an ideal way for her to spend her first night at home. It would've been nice if she could've spent it with her new husband and stepson.

By the time she unhitched the horse, washed her hands and changed out of her clothes, she slipped into bed just as Jacob's alarm clock sounded. He rolled over, kissed her, and in two minutes she told him about baby Sam's arrival and that was all she remembered. The next thing she knew, she woke up alone with the warm sun streaming through her room. Knowing Micah would be at Anne's, and considering the time she had gotten home, she closed her eyes to catch up on the many hours of lost sleep.

MAY WOKE HAVING BEEN unable to sleep all night. She'd been tossing and turning and worrying that she would never marry if she didn't do something soon. She had to find a way to make William notice her, but she had to be careful to make the right move. May waited until she heard her mother rattling around in the kitchen and her father leaving for work before she went down to talk to her mother. "Can I make you breakfast, *Mamm?*" May slumped into a chair.

Her mother was sitting at the kitchen table drinking coffee. "Good morning. You must want *me* to make you breakfast because you're sitting down."

"I can stand up if you want me to make it."

Her mother laughed. "I just made your *vadder* some eggs. I'll make you some if you want."

"Yeah, that'll be fine. *Denke, Mamm.*"

Her mother drained the last of her coffee and then placed the mug down on the table. "Don't forget it's washing day today."

"I won't. How can I forget something as important as that?"

As her mother whisked the eggs with a fork, she looked up at May. "Not too happy this morning?"

"I'm fine." She smiled not wanting her mother to

know she was miserable and churning inside. *Mamm* would only tell her she was being silly and had nothing to worry about. Either that, or she'd tell her to pray about her problem. That was her answer for everything, but sometimes advice and guidance were what was needed. That's why God put mothers on the earth, May thought, but there was no point in telling her mother that.

While her mother poured the eggs into the pan, May made herself a cup of coffee and then sat down with it. She stared into the dark steaming liquid wondering if she could slip away during the day to see Abigail. She was a widow with a child and, somehow, she'd gotten Timothy to agree to marry her. Abigail had fallen for Timothy and she might be able to offer advice on marrying a second time. Most of the younger widowers and widows in the community married again. It was only the older ones who didn't. And that meant William was most likely to get married at some point and she had to ensure she was the one he chose.

Her mother placed a plate of scrambled eggs and toast down in front of her.

"*Denke, Mamm.*"

"You're welcome."

May looked up at her mother. "Have you eaten already?"

Mamm slumped into a chair. "I'm just not hungry."

"Why not? Sick of your own cooking?"

The corners of her mother's eyes crinkled as she

fought against a giggle. "Don't be cheeky. I'm just feeling a bit off this morning."

"Why don't you go back to bed?" If her mother went back to bed, she wouldn't notice if she sneaked off right after doing the washing.

"I'll be okay. I might have a rest after lunch if I'm still feeling tired."

"Would you mind if I left home after the washing? I'll only be gone an hour or so."

"Hmm, every time you say that you end up being gone the whole rest of the day." She shook her head. "And then there's the washing to be done."

May sighed. *"Jah,* that's what I meant — can I go after I pin the washing out? I'll be back in time to bring it in when it's dry and before the cold afternoon air gets to it."

"Where are you off to that's so important?"

"I just want to visit Abigail, seeing I'm lonely now since April's gone." She pushed her bottom lip into a pity-me-pout.

"Sure. Everyone needs a friend. I've been worried about you. I'll tell you what. Why don't you go whenever you're ready and I'll do the washing?"

"Nee, Mamm, not when you're feeling ill. I'll leave as soon as I pin it out. Okay?"

Her mother nodded. "Don't hurry back. You young people should have some fun."

"I don't think visiting Abigail will exactly be fun, but okay."

"While you're out that way could you get some things from the markets?"

"Sure."

Her mother started telling her what they needed and when she saw the glazed look on May's face, she said, "I guess it's enough that I'll write out a list."

CHAPTER 4

ON HER WAY to the markets, May passed Jacob and Rebecca's new house. The temptation was too strong to resist. She wasn't going to knock on the door in case Rebecca was asleep, but if she just happened to look in the window and see Rebecca awake, it would be a perfect opportunity to talk with her about William.

When she pulled the buggy into the driveway, she noticed Anne at the back of the house with baby Micah in her arms. Anne looked at her, waved, and walked to the buggy while May secured her horse.

"Hello. May, isn't it?"

"That's right." May was delighted Anne hadn't confused her with April. But, she figured, only because Anne hadn't been there long enough to know them as 'the twins.' They weren't identical twins and the only thing similar about them was their coloring, but that didn't stop people from confusing the two of them. "Is Rebecca home?"

"She arrived home very late last night — or it could've been the early hours of the morning. Anyway, she hasn't stirred."

"That's right. Mary had the *boppli?*"

"*Jah,* she had a *bu.*"

"Oh, that's *wunderbaar.* I'm happy for them." May glanced at the house. "I was hoping to talk with Rebecca. Never mind. Could you tell her I stopped by?"

"*Jah,* I'll do that."

"*Denke.*" May's gaze dropped to little Micah. "He's a sweet little boy."

"*Jah,* he is."

"Rebecca and Jacob are blessed to have you to look after him when she's called out overnight."

"And I'm pleased to be wanted."

May smiled and said goodbye to Anne. Things had definitely worked out for Rebecca and also for her brother, Timothy. Perhaps God was blessing the bishop's entire family. The bishop might spend more time in prayer than everyone else in the community and that would explain why they were blessed, May figured.

May left Rebecca's house and took a detour to stop by Abigail's *haus* on her way to the markets. She walked up to the front door and knocked gently in case Abigail's daughter, Ferris, was asleep. By this time, it was mid-morning.

Abigail opened the front door. "Good morning, May. Come in."

"Denke." When she walked in the door, she saw young Ferris playing in the middle of the living room floor. "I hope I'm not disturbing you."

"Not at all. It's nice having visitors. Would you like a cup of hot tea?"

"I would, *denke."* May followed Abigail into the kitchen. "You just bought this *haus?"*

"I did. Technically, I'm in the process of buying it. It needs some work, but Timothy's doing it for me. It'll soon be his place too." They both sat down at the table. "It does need a lot of fixing, but Timothy's happy to do that in between his jobs."

"He's working now?"

"Jah, for himself. He's got quite a lot of work already and his first client was a large real estate firm. He's also going to be doing a little work on Jacob and Rebecca's new *haus,* and he's got plenty of work lined up for the future."

"That *is* good to hear."

"Oh, the tea." Abigail got up and filled the teakettle, placed it on the gas stove and lit the burner.

"I need to ask your advice about something if that's all right, Abigail? Woman to woman."

Abigail moved back to her seat. "Of course. If I can help, I will."

"What do you think a widower would be looking for in a *fraa?"*

Abigail's eyebrows rose. "You like a widower?"

"I do. Is that so shocking?"

"Nee, not at all, but I just thought that…" She shook her head. "I don't know."

May leaned forward. "Please tell me what you're thinking."

"I would've thought that a beautiful girl like you could have any man she wanted, and marrying a widower wouldn't be an easy choice to make."

Smiling now, May was pleased with the compliment. "But you were a widow yourself, and with a child. The man I like lost his wife a few years ago and he has two young daughters. Not as young as Ferris. They're a little older."

"And you like him?"

"Very much so, and I'm wondering what he would be looking for in a woman. Would he think I'm too young, or something? That's my concern."

"I don't know. What's the age difference?"

"I'm not sure but at least ten years."

Abigail exhaled heavily. "That is quite a bit."

"What's the age difference between you and Timothy?"

"We're the same age — we have the same birthday in the same year, and everything. So just a few hours difference."

"Wow. That's almost unheard of."

"I know. It is a big coincidence. He'd never get away

34

with forgetting my birthday." She giggled. "And I would probably remember his."

May smiled and she could see that Abigail and she could become good friends. "I thought you two were around the same age, but I thought you might be a little older since you have Ferris. I thought you might be one of those women who looks really young."

The kettle whistled and Abigail jumped to her feet. "Hot tea? Or would you prefer *kaffe?*"

"*Jah*, tea please."

"Milk and sugar?"

"Two sugars and just a dash of milk."

"Okay."

When they both had their tea in front of them, May leaned back and took a sip. "Ferris has been good playing out there by herself."

Abigail stood up and looked around the corner. "She's playing with blocks Timothy made for her. She'd play with them all day if she could." Abigail sat back down.

"Is it strange to be marrying for a second time?"

"I never thought I'd marry again, not so soon anyway. It was something I thought I might do many years down the road." She touched the strings of her *kapp*, almost as though she was nervous. "Things were different with my first husband, very different. But that's a story for another day. You didn't come here to talk about me."

She had that right, but the story might give May some insight. "You can tell me." May took another mouthful of tea.

"Another day. I don't want to think about that now. I just want my mind on my wedding to Timothy and getting everything ready for it."

"Would you like some help?"

"I'd love some. Hannah's organizing everything, so I'll let her know you offered, okay?"

"Certainly. I'll do anything I can. I'm sorry I've left things so late. I should've volunteered earlier since your wedding is only days away."

"That's fine. Hannah will find something for you to do." Abigail narrowed her eyes. "How well do you know this man?"

"Well enough to like him. I wouldn't even call him a friend though, sadly. I've been too shy to talk to him."

"And his daughters?"

"Not that well. I don't want to be too obvious. I guess that's the first step, isn't it?"

"What impressed me first about Timothy was how well he got along with Ferris. Ferris absolutely adores him and, through Ferris, Timothy broke down the walls around my heart."

"Is that so?"

"It is. Do his daughters still go to school?"

"They do. One is eight, I think, and the other's about ten."

Abigail took a sip of tea and then placed her cup

gently onto the saucer. "Hmm. I was having dinner the other night with Timothy's family and, as you know, his *vadder* is the bishop."

"*Jah*, I know that."

"Well, they had someone else there for dinner, the schoolteacher, Deborah Morris. And I happen to know she's looking for a capable assistant. Is that something you'd feel like you might like to do? I don't think it'll be a paid job. I think it was a volunteer position because they already pay Deborah and they were talking about the lack of funds available for extra help for Deborah. You could volunteer your help — it might only be just a couple of hours a day."

"And you're thinking that's a good way to get to know the children and from there get closer to William?"

"William, that's his name?"

May put her fingertips over her mouth and giggled. "Whoops. I hadn't told you his name yet, had I?"

Abigail shook her head and giggled along with her. "Don't worry, I won't tell anybody. I probably would have to tell Timothy if he asked me outright, but he wouldn't because he knows nothing about it. I'm sure your secret is safe."

"Whew." May wiped pretend sweat off her brow.

"I think that's exactly what you should do. Talk with Deborah about helping her at school and if it doesn't work out, what have you lost?"

"Nothing."

Abigail nodded. "And if she agrees to you volunteering, you'll be doing a good thing anyway, helping out with the children."

"Exactly. *Denke*, Abigail." Feeling much better, May took another sip of hot tea.

When they heard the rattling of a wagon, Abigail jumped up and look out the window. "Here is Timothy now. Sometimes he leaves the wagon here and takes my buggy because it's faster into town."

May jumped up. "I should go."

"*Nee*, don't. You stay there. I'll say hi to Timothy and I'll be back in one minute. Will you watch Ferris for me?"

"Of course."

While Abigail rushed out to see Timothy, May sat down on the rug with Ferris and helped her arrange blocks. She could hear muffled voices outside, but couldn't hear what was said.

A few minutes later, Abigail came back inside. "He's going in a minute. He said to say hi but he's too busy to come in and say hello properly. He didn't even have time to say hello to Ferris."

"That's fine. *Denke* for all your advice. Who shall I see about the job at the school? Deborah or the school board?"

"Deborah. Bishop Elmer said she has the choice."

"I will see her as soon as I can."

After May had finished her tea, she continued into

town to do the shopping. Since Abigail's wedding was in a couple of days, she decided to wait and talk to Deborah then.

CHAPTER 5

AFTER REBECCA WAS AWAKE ENOUGH to make herself something to eat, she did so and then headed to Anne's portion of the house. The door was open so she stuck her head through. "Anne," she called softly.

Anne walked out from the kitchen area drying her hands on a tea towel. "There you are. I heard Mary had a boy."

"She did. And all went well."

"That's good to hear. We've all been keeping her in our prayers. I suppose you're looking for Micah?"

"*Jah*. He's not asleep again, is he?"

Anne giggled. "I'm afraid he is."

Rebecca sighed. "Would it be all right to leave him here while I visited a couple of people just quickly?"

"Of course it will. Leave him here all day if you want. I'm not going anywhere."

"*Denke*, Anne. Do you need anything while I'm out?"

"Nee. I'm fine. I shop once a fortnight and get exactly what I need and a little extra. Where are you going? Oh, I forgot to tell you that May stopped by yesterday. No wait, it could've been early this morning." Anne shook her head. "One day runs into another around here."

"I know exactly what you mean. Did she tell you what she wanted?"

"Nee, but she looked a little disturbed."

"Well, I'll call in to see her after I talk to Timothy. I haven't seen him since I've been back."

"It must've been a shock to learn he was getting married."

"It was, since he only met Abigail a few weeks ago. At my wedding, in fact."

"Ah, that's so romantic," Anne said.

Rebecca fixed a smile on her face and nodded. She didn't agree with what Anne said, but neither did she want Anne to know that she wasn't happy about her brother's sudden marriage. "I'll try not to be too long."

"Take your time. Micah is okay here."

"Denke, Anne. I'll just peep in and see him." Rebecca headed to the room Anne had set up as Micah's room. She leaned down to see him fast asleep. She had to stop herself from kissing his chubby soft cheek. Hopefully later today, she'd be able to spend some time with him.

SEEING IT WAS NEARLY LUNCHTIME, Rebecca's best guess

42

was that she might be able to find Timothy at home. When she pulled into the driveway, she was glad to see his horse and buggy. It would be so much easier to talk to him there rather than at Abigail's place.

When she walked into the kitchen, she saw Timothy had just finished a bowl of food and was wiping his mouth.

"Hi, where's *Mamm?*"

"Hi there." Timothy stood up, rushed to her and hugged her. "You're back."

"*Jah*, and Mary had the *boppli* last night so I'm trying to recover from lack of sleep." She gave a little giggle.

"Yeah, I heard they had a boy."

"That's right. Where's *Mamm?*" she repeated.

"I don't know. She went somewhere with *Dat.*"

"Ah."

"Is there anything wrong?"

"*Nee.* It's just that I want to talk with you alone."

He quickly looked at the clock on the wall. "Right now?"

"Do you have to leave?"

"I've got about five minutes to spare."

"Good. Sit down. This will only take a few minutes."

"Ow. What have I done?"

She made herself comfortable on the chair. "I come back to hear you're getting married."

Timothy chuckled. "That's right. Abigail's the lucky woman. *Mamm* said you met her at your wedding."

"*Jah,* just a couple of weeks ago, and 'met her' is all. I

don't know much about her and I don't know how you could, either. You haven't had time to get to know her properly."

He leaned back in the chair. "Listen, I wasn't too happy about you getting married to Jacob either, if you recall, but I trusted in your judgement. Can't you do the same for me?"

"I just don't see what the rush is."

"It's called love and we want to be together as soon as possible. Surely you understand that much?"

Rebecca exhaled deeply. "I just don't want you to get married and learn you've made a terrible mistake."

"Neither do I and that won't happen. Trust me."

She shook her head. "I hope you know what you're doing. I just don't see what the rush is."

"You've already said that."

She rubbed her forehead trying to think of something she could say to make him see sense.

"It's this way. I'm excited to start a new chapter in my life, one that includes Abigail and her daughter, Ferris. I'm over the moon in love with this woman. I never knew I could feel like this about another person. And, I know she's not perfect, but neither am I. Don't forget, she lived here in this house for a while, so we did have time to talk together. Once you get to know Abigail and Ferris you'll love them too."

"I was shocked to hear it, that's all. At the wedding, you were all excited about taking over my room and I had in my mind you'd be here for a while longer. Aside from that, I guess I thought you would marry a girl from our own community."

"I did too, but it didn't work out like that. It doesn't really matter, does it?"

"*Nee*, you're right, it doesn't. Jacob comes from a different community as well." She shook her head. "It doesn't matter. I just want to make sure you'll be happy."

"I'll be more than happy. You should follow me over to Abigail's *haus* now. I'm doing some work on it this afternoon."

"I would, but I'm going to see May."

"Okay. We'll have you over for dinner soon. You and Jacob."

"And Micah and Anne?"

He chuckled. "Sure. Everyone."

"We're kind of a team."

He leaned forward. "It's called a family."

Rebecca laughed. "I would like to know Abigail better."

"And you will." He pushed his chair out and stood up. "Did you know I'm working for myself now?"

"That's great. Is there enough work?"

"*Jah*. Remember that real estate agency that sacked me?"

"I do."

"Well, they're one of my main customers."

"Oh, Timothy. That's wonderful."

"Abigail inspired me and gave me confidence in

myself to do it, and so did Samuel Kauffman."

"That's so good. I'm happy for you."

"Are you sticking around?"

"*Nee.* I'll leave too." Rebecca was curious to know why May had stopped by to see her. She'd already told May she'd visit her soon.

As soon as Rebecca pulled her buggy to a stop in May's driveway, May came running out toward her with her hands holding her dress bunched up at either side. "Rebecca, hi. Did Anne tell you I came to see you?"

"*Jah*, she did." Rebecca stepped down and walked closer to May. "Is everything okay?"

"It is." A breathless May glanced back at her house. "Can we take a little walk? I've something to say and I don't want *Mamm* to overhear."

"Sure."

Once they were a little distance from the house, May began, "The reason I wanted to talk to you was to see if you could help me out."

"Sure. What with?"

"Remember what I told you just before the phone call about Mary? I like a widower, William Bronstein, and I wanted your advice."

"Oh, William, *jah.* You had told me that much just before Samuel called."

"*Jah.* Don't tell anyone, will you?"

"I won't. What kind of advice are you looking for?"

"He's a widower and you've just married Jacob, so I thought you'd know what a man who's been married before would be looking for in a new wife."

"That's a hard one. It could be different for everyone."

"I didn't think of that."

"I don't know William. How did *you* get to know him so well?"

May shook her head. "I don't know him either. Not really."

Rebecca stood still and May stopped walking. "What is it about him that attracts you?"

May shrugged her shoulders. "He just seems so sure of himself. And I like how attentive he is to his daughters. I also like the way he looks."

"I think the first thing you need to do is get to know him. Just be yourself around him and don't be nervous."

"I'll try. I'm no good at the 'don't be nervous' part, though. Deborah needs help at school and I'm going to ask if she'll consider me for the job. I guess I'd have some interaction with parents."

Rebecca smiled. "That sounds like a good plan."

"I hope she accepts me."

"She will. I'm sure."

May smiled at Rebecca and then glanced back at the house. "You've made me feel more confident. Do you want to come in and say hello to *Mamm?*"

"*Jah,* let's go."

CHAPTER 6

MAY WAS PLEASED to be going to Abigail and Timothy's wedding at the bishop's house because she would see William again. There was a buzz of excitement in the air because everyone was pleased for the bishop and Hannah's oldest son to be getting married.

Sadly for Abigail, none of her family members were there because they lived too far away. The only member of her family in attendance was her daughter, Ferris. After the actual wedding ceremony had taken place, May helped the women bring the food out to the trestle tables. When she'd taken several trips to and from the kitchen, she caught sight of the school teacher, Deborah. As soon as the workload slowed and Hannah had her back turned, May took the opportunity to slip away to speak with Deborah.

"May," a male voice sounded before she got there. She turned around to see Jeff.

"Hi, Jeff."

"What did you think of the wedding?"

"Truly spectacular." It wasn't. It was much the same as any other Amish wedding, but of course she couldn't say that.

"I thought so too. It's funny Rebecca got married and then Timothy got married so soon after, to—"

"Not really. People get married all the time." She stared at Jeff and he smiled at her.

"You know what I mean, though. She married a widower and—."

She interrupted him, "I have no idea what you're talking about, Jeff. Excuse me, I need to talk to someone before I lose sight of them."

After she'd taken a step away from him, he asked, "Who?"

"Just someone." Quickly, she turned aside and headed to Deborah who was just sitting down to a plate of food.

"Hi, Deborah."

"Hello, May." Deborah was in her early thirties and had never married. She was a plain looking woman with greenish brown eyes and medium ashy-brown hair that intensified the sallow tone of her skin.

May sat next to her. "Somebody said you're looking for someone to help you out at school. Is that right?"

"I am. Is that something you'd like to do?"

"*Jah.*" May offered a bright smile.

"Really?" Deborah's lips curved upward and May

considered how much nicer she looked when she smiled.

"*Jah.* I was quite good at school work and I would like to help out if I can."

"It won't be a paid job and it's only an hour or two a day to aid the children in their reading. I don't have the time to listen to them individually during school hours."

"I would love that more than anything, and I do have the time. And I don't need payment."

"Perfect. Would you want to try it out starting Monday?"

"I certainly would. *Denke,* Deborah."

Deborah smiled once more and then picked up her fork. "Come on Monday and we'll see how it works out for both of us, shall we?"

"*Jah,* I'll be the best teacher's assistant you ever had." Deborah gave a small nod and then other people sat down at the table. "I'll be there early on Monday."

"Okay. I'm usually there from seven thirty onward, so you can come whenever you like. School starts at nine. It might be a good idea if you come early the first day, so we can discuss things before the children get there."

"It'll be well before nine."

"*Denke,* May."

May left Deborah and headed back to the food tables while looking around for William. And then she saw him in the corner of the yard. She reached over and took a plate then began to fill it with food. When she looked back up at William, she saw his daughters walking away from him heading toward Deborah. Then, to her dismay, William followed. May stopped still.

"You gonna move on?" someone asked her.

She realized she was holding up the line of people who were moving around the food table. *"Ach jah,* sorry. Daydreaming."

When she'd put the last thing on her plate, she was upset to see William and his girls sitting with Deborah. It was a good idea of Abigail's to be a teacher's assistant, but she hoped she wasn't too late. It seemed pretty obvious Deborah was also interested in William. That was something she needed to find out for certain and come Monday, she'd do just that.

Now, she was no longer interested in the food piled high on her plate, but she had to force it down. No one would appreciate her wasting so much food. She chomped her way through the meal, mouthful by mouthful, and when she was finished, she was relieved to walk over and put the empty plate with all the others. Then she carried an armful of dishes to the kitchen to help out.

When she came back out of the house, Jeff was helping himself to a second round of food. She walked over to him. "Hungry?"

"Not really, but the food's so good."

She laughed. "Don't you get fed at home?"

"I do, but the food's not as good as this. Just don't tell my *Mamm* I said that."

"I won't. You know what you were talking about before about Timothy getting married and Rebecca getting married just recently?"

He frowned. *"Jah?"*

"Did you notice both of them married people who've been married before?"

"I did, that's what I was trying to say to you earlier and you wouldn't let me speak to the end of the thought."

"Oh, I see. Do you think it's a bit weird?"

"Not weird, exactly, but it's a little unusual. You think that's a trend? A new marriage trend?" He laughed.

"It could be." She folded her arms across her chest. "Is it hard marrying someone who's been married before, or is it easier or harder to marry someone who's never been married?"

"I think it would be okay to marry a widow, but I personally wouldn't want to. It's not ideal, not for me."

"I suppose, but what if you fell in love with someone who was a widow?"

His mouth twisted into a smile that lit up his face. "Well, that's the only reason for marriage, isn't that right?"

"That's true. No one has said anything bad about Timothy or Rebecca's marriages, have they?"

"If they have, I haven't heard."

"Good, that's good." When she heard the cries of a newborn, she turned around and saw Mary. "Mary's here with the new *boppli*. I'll have to talk to you later." She rushed to Mary, who'd just sat and was placing her baby across her lap. May crouched down beside her. "Mary, congratulations on your *boppli*."

"*Denke*."

"I'm so excited. Can I see him?"

Mary smiled and picked him up so May could see his face.

"He's beautiful, just *wunderbaar,* and so small."

"He is beautiful."

May cleared her throat. "This is your second marriage, isn't it?"

"That's right. I was married before, but he died."

"That's right, I remember now." May had heard the rumors. He hadn't exactly been the best husband in the world. In fact, he might have been the worst. His behavior had been swept under the rug like so many things in their community.

Mary positioned her baby back where he'd been before, resting across her lap. "Why do you ask?"

"I'm just wondering what it's like to marry a second time, that's all."

Mary shook her head. "I can't compare the two marriages. I thought I was in love with my first husband leading up to the marriage, but things went dreadfully wrong. It was such a mismatch. I never dreamed it would turn out as bad as it did." She shook her head and her bottom lip trembled slightly and May knew just how awful that relationship must've been. "It wasn't a good marriage." Mary gulped.

"I'm sorry to hear that."

"With Samuel, everything is perfect. Well, it's not perfect." She looked brighter. "But it's pretty close to it."

"That's good. Good to hear. And you've got this beautiful little *bu* and you can share your love with him, and you've got Lois too."

"That's right. We've been doubly blessed."

May looked over at William, who was still sitting with the school teacher, and wondered what his first marriage had been like. She barely remembered his wife, Nita, as May had been a young teenager when she'd died.

"Why are you asking, May?"

"Um, I've just got a few things to figure out that's all."

"Like what?"

"Just about life, love, and marriage."

"Second marriages in particular?"

May nodded.

"Am I guessing right that you might like somebody who's been married before?"

"That's right."

Mary looked around them. "And from the direction your eyes keep wandering, would that 'somebody' be William?"

May looked down and giggled, feeling her face flush with heat. "That's right, but no one knows."

"He doesn't know?"

"Nee. He doesn't. How could I ever tell him? He barely knows me and I'm so much younger."

"I think he'd be pleased to know you like him in that way."

She was pleased to get Mary's advice. "Do you think so?"

"Definitely."

The baby opened his mouth and yelled loudly. Mary changed him to an upright position. He was quiet for a moment and then he yowled even louder. "If you'll excuse me, I'll have to go inside the *haus* and feed him."

"Okay, and *denke,* Mary."

"Anytime." She gave May a big smile. "Maybe in a couple of weeks when I'm less tired I can have the two of you over for dinner?"

"Really? Me and William?"

Mary nodded.

"I'd love that."

"I'll arrange something."

"Denke, so much, Mary. Only when you've recovered from the birth."

"I'm blessed to have Freda because she does the cooking. And we'll have dinner anyway, with or without guests."

May smiled at her. It was such a blessing for her to have help in the home due to Samuel being wealthy.

56

May watched Mary walk into the house with her baby cradled in her arms.

May looked around at William once more. Before she spotted him, she saw Jeff heading her way. As a way of escape, she jumped up and hurried to the kitchen to help out.

When she walked in, she heard Aunt Agatha say to the crowd of women in the kitchen, "Has everyone heard the latest?"

All eyes turned to the elderly woman.

"Nee, what is it?" Hannah asked.

"It's Karen. She's expecting again and it's another set of twins."

Hannah's face beamed. "Oh, she's so blessed having another set of twins. She's doubling her family, and so quickly."

"It's not that quickly," Aunt Agatha said, with her nose in the air. "Her pregnancies were quite a distance apart."

"But still, that's such good news. I must find her and congratulate her." Hannah tossed her tea towel aside.

Hannah went to walk away and Aunt Agatha grabbed her hand. "Wait. It's a secret, no one must know. Don't say anything to Karen until she or someone else says something to you." Aunt Agatha said to all the women. "That goes for all of you."

Hannah stepped back. "Oh, I didn't know."

"That's why I'm telling you all now."

Hannah gave Aunt Agatha a smile and walked past her. "I'll just talk to Karen and won't mention a thing."

Within one minute, the kitchen was nearly empty. May didn't know why having twins was such a big deal. Sometimes it wasn't fun to be a twin at all. There were many bad things about it. May guessed everyone had gone to speak with Karen hoping she'd reveal her news. The only person left besides May was Rebecca, who had her hands in sudsy water at the kitchen sink. She obviously hadn't run out with the others because she was the midwife and already knew Karen's news.

"Hi, Rebecca."

"Hello, May. How are you enjoying the wedding?"

"Good, and you must be happy your older *bruder* is married now, just like you?"

Rebecca giggled.

May realized what a silly thing she'd just said and laughed too. "Do you know any news?" May asked.

"I don't think so. Like what?" Rebecca was playing dumb about Karen's news. "Are you talking about the barn raising next week?"

"I wasn't, but now that you mention it, are you going?" May picked up a tea towel and started wiping up.

"I plan to and, come to think of it, that would be a good time for you to see more of William." Rebecca was right.

"If I'm free, I'll go."

"They start early and finish late. It would be a

perfect time to talk with William because the men have to stop to drink and eat, and then you could speak with him."

"Well, that is a thought, but I might have a job at the school."

"Is that so?"

"It's just a couple of hours a day. I'm trying it out on Monday."

"Perfect. If you're working at school on that day you can do it before or after. You could come to the barn raising before or after that, I mean."

May twitched her lips. "Will you help me with William?"

"Of course I will. What are you planning?"

"Nothing apart from getting the courage to speak with him. Mary said she'd have me and him over for dinner when she recovers a bit more from the birth."

"That'll be a good start."

"*Jah,* and I'll be seeing him at the school when he collects his girls." She hoped he'd be the one to collect them. She hadn't considered the possibility someone else might do that. They lived too far from the school for the girls to walk. She'd find out soon enough.

CHAPTER 7

ONE BY ONE, the teacher sent the children over to May in the corner of the room, so they could read out loud to her. Deborah told them all it was good practice to read aloud. May was to listen to them for ten minutes each. The first child who came to her was William's oldest, Ivy.

"Now don't be nervous, just read as though I'm not here." May smiled at her and patted the chair next to her.

"Okay." Ivy sat down on the chair, opened her book, took a deep breath and started reading. She made a few errors, then went back and corrected herself.

After ten minutes, May reached out for the book. "Okay, time's up. That's very good, Ivy."

"*Denke*, Miss May. Is that all for today?"

May marked the page, closed the book and handed

it back to Ivy with a nod. "That's all. Now tell your *schweschder* to come to me for her turn at reading."

Ivy leaned in and whispered, "She's not very good at it."

May whispered back, "That's why she needs to practice."

Ivy smiled at her. Then she walked away and tapped her little sister, Grace, on the shoulder and pointed to May. Grace gave May a big smile and walked over to her clutching her reading book.

"What book do you have for me today?"

She held the book up. "It's a story about Joseph and his coat."

"That sounds interesting. Joseph and his coat of many colors. Start when you're ready and don't be nervous."

Grace read quickly barely pausing for breath. She made errors but May didn't want to destroy her confidence by pointing them out. She thought it would be better to wait until Grace was more used to her before correcting the mistakes. When Grace's ten minutes was up, May told her she'd read well and asked her to fetch the next child. May continued like that until the teacher rang the lunch bell.

When the children had gone outside, Deborah walked over to her. "How do you like it?"

"I like it a lot. Very fulfilling. I can see why someone would become a teacher."

"I'm glad to hear it. That's all for today *denke*, May.

Unless you'd like to stay on for the rest of the day so you can see what I do?"

She wanted to stay and then she would see William when he came to fetch his children at the end of the day. "I might stay on just for today if that's okay because my *mudder* is not expecting me home until late."

"Perfect. How did the children do with their reading?"

"You've done a good job with them. I was surprised how well they read." She gave Deborah a big smile.

"They are fairly good."

May added, "And the more they practice the better they will be."

"That's right. And we're grateful for your help. Did you bring any food with you, May?"

"I do have a little something in the buggy."

"Perfect — bring it in and we can eat lunch together while we watch the children."

WHEN THE SCHOOL day had ended, May waited with Deborah outside of the one-room schoolhouse. Some children walked home, but most were collected in buggies. May was anxious to know whether Grace and Ivy would be collected by William or whether he'd have someone else collect them.

She didn't have long to wait because Deborah took off at quite a pace without saying a word. May followed the direction she was headed and saw she was following behind Ivy and Grace who were heading to a buggy. When William got out and talked to Deborah, May didn't like it one bit. Deborah had talked to him at the wedding and now he was talking to her at school. It seemed to May she'd left things too late.

If she'd never helped out at the school, she wouldn't have found out that Deborah liked William. Deborah Morris was more William's age, anyway. May knew there was no use both of them talking to William at school like Deborah was now doing. May walked a few steps toward them and then called out, "Excuse me, Deborah, is it all right if I go home now?"

Deborah swung around. "Of course, May. I appreciate your help today."

"You're welcome." She saw William smiling at her and felt a spark of hope. She gave him a wave. "Hi, William."

He lifted his hand and waved. "Hi, May. Have you been working at the school?"

"I have today and if Deborah thinks I've done a good job, I'll keep doing that a couple of hours a day."

"Good to hear."

"Bye, Deborah,

"Thanks again, May. And I would like your help again tomorrow if you're able,"

"I'd love to."

"See you then. You don't have to come so early tomorrow."

"Okay, bye."

"Bye," Deborah said before she turned back around to talk further with William. May headed inside to fetch the container in which she'd brought her lunch, and then she walked out to her buggy. She glanced William's way and saw them still talking and the girls sitting in the buggy waiting to go home.

As she drove away, she realized how tired she was from the day even though she hadn't done anything physical. She blinked hard fighting the drowsiness. Anyway, if she fell asleep, she knew Nigel would find his way home. There were no major roads or intersections to cross.

When May's house came into view, a taxi was pulling out of the driveway. There was no one in it but the driver, and that meant they had a visitor.

It could've been one of her mother's friends visiting. A couple of them didn't have buggies, so it was likely *Mamm* would ask her to drive them home. Before she unhitched the buggy, she opened the back door to inquire whether someone would need to be taken home. She couldn't believe her eyes when she saw who was sitting at the kitchen table.

"May!"

Her twin sister ran toward her with arms wide open.

CHAPTER 8

THE TWINS, April and May, hugged.

"April, what are you doing here?" May looked April up and down. She looked well. Then she looked at her belly to see if she might've come home to tell them she was expecting. Her belly was as flat as a pancake. "Where's Philip?"

April stared at her. "Philip's still at home. He didn't want to come."

That was something May couldn't understand. Why get married and go somewhere alone? If May married she'd stay home with her husband if he wasn't able to go somewhere or didn't want to. "What are you doing here without him?"

April looked over at their mother, and when May looked at the expression on *Mamm's* face, she could see *Mamm* thought it odd as well.

"What's going on?" May asked. "Someone please tell me something?"

"There's nothing going on. I've just come for a little vacation, that's all." April sat back down.

May slumped into the chair beside her. "A vacation without your husband?"

"Yeah, why not? I need a little break and he said it was fine, so here I am." April leaned forward. "Now tell me everything that's been going on with you."

"Wait until I unhitch the buggy."

"I'll come out with you." The two girls left their mother in the kitchen. As May unhitched the buggy, April made a startling confession. "My marriage isn't what I'd hoped. I thought my life would begin once I married and now I feel as though it's ended. It was a mistake to marry him."

May straightened up and stared at her twin sister. "Why? Does he beat you or something, like Mary's first husband did?"

"Nothing like that, not at all. He just ignores me most of the time. I might as well not even be there. I might as well just be a chair in the room rather than his *fraa*." April looked down at the dirt underneath her feet and shook her head. "That's all the notice Philip takes of me."

"But you were in love before you married, weren't you?"

"I guess so. I don't know. I thought so." April shrugged her shoulders. "What is love anyway? Is it just a feeling or is it something real? I don't believe in love anymore."

"Love between a man and a woman should be like you can't survive unless you see that person."

April giggled. "Aha! Who are you in love with this week?"

May ignored April's cruel jab. "Don't tell anybody, but I like William."

"William?"

May nodded. *"Jah."*

"The only William I can think of is William Bronstein with Ivy and Grace."

"That's him."

"Yeah, I can see you two together. Although, he is a little old for you, don't you think?"

May was pleased April hadn't made a joke out of her secret longing for the much older man. "Not that old. Not too old."

"I would consider him too old for me and that means for you too."

"True love doesn't recognize age."

April giggled. "I've missed you so much." She put her arm around May and pulled her close to her. "I'm not having any fun anymore. That's it. That's what I'm missing, fun."

May broke free by squirming out of her embrace. "Yeah, but sometimes what you call fun ends up landing you in a whole heap of trouble."

"That's untrue, it doesn't."

May finished rubbing down her horse and put him back in his stall. She didn't comment on what her sister had said. April liked to make trouble, she truly did, and it wasn't fun for May being dragged into the messes April made.

"I heard a rumor, something I know you'll be interested in."

May dusted off her hands as they headed to the house. "What kind of agreement?"

"I didn't say an agreement, I said a rumor. You must be in love. Clean out your eyes if you want to hear it."

May giggled. "You mean your ears."

"Ah, *jah*. We're just as silly as each other. Anyway, do you want to know it or not?"

"I shouldn't listen to rumors."

April held up her hands with her palms facing the sky. "Neither should anyone."

"Well, what is it?" May couldn't resist knowing.

"It's a rumor about Mary."

"It's true. She's just had a *boppli* and they've called him Sam after Samuel."

April shook her head. "I know that, silly. That's a fact, not a rumor. You wanna know what I heard?" April stopped in her tracks and May stopped too.

"What?"

"I heard Lois is really Mary's child."

May thought for a moment. "*Nee*, she's Beth's, Samuel's *schweschder*. Everyone knows that." May shook her head. "You call me silly. You're the only one who is." May giggled.

April shook her head. "Karen and Mary were best friends with Beth."

"So what?"

"Mary's first husband died, some even say she killed him." April's eyes opened wide.

"You shouldn't say that, April. You know that's not true. That's cruel."

"Not really. He was a drunkard and a wife-beater. I heard she had bruises all over from him." April shrugged her shoulders.

"I think the problem was that he converted to the Amish way of life and wasn't born into it. Then, he regretted it deeply and was out drinking most nights. After he died, everyone found out about the way he'd treated Mary, but it was never mentioned apart from whispers here and there. You shouldn't repeat what you hear."

"Whatever! Do you want to hear the scandal or not?"

May knew she should say no, but didn't. "What is it?"

"Mary's first husband died. He probably jumped in front of that truck because his life was miserable with Mary. Who knows? Anyway, he dies, she's pregnant and doesn't want to raise the child by herself. So, what will she do? Anyone else would keep the child, but not Mary. She gives the baby to Beth because, it's said, Beth couldn't have one of her own. There must've been something wrong with her. Anyway, maybe Beth took advantage of Mary and bribed her, or paid for the child. Anyway, both Beth and Mary went somewhere else in the last months of 'Beth's pregnancy,' and that in itself is highly suspicious. Anyway, Beth ended up with Mary's baby and raised her until both she and her husband were struck down dead by *Gott's* wrath."

"Oh, April, that's awful. Beth and her husband were killed in an accident. Why would you say *Gott's* wrath?"

"Because maybe they stole the *boppli* from Mary. *Gott* was angry and He made things right by giving Lois back to Mary." April gave a nod. "So there."

May rubbed her head with the overload of information. "And then what do you say happened?"

"After they died, Samuel took Lois."

"We know that's true. Go on."

"Mary stepped in to help him look after Lois, and Samuel allowed it. Maybe Samuel was in on it all along. Anyway, Samuel and Mary got married, most likely to cover up their secret."

"Mary and Samuel are very much in love."

April shrugged her shoulders. "Who knows? Maybe they are and maybe it's all an act, but they're keeping a secret and I think it should come out."

May's heart sank. "It's just a vicious rumor. Don't get involved. You know what happened last time you made something up?"

"*Jah*, but this time it's true."

"Why do you believe it?"

April breathed out heavily. "Have you seen how Lois's hair matches Mary's, exactly?"

May thought back to the reddish strawberry blonde hair they both shared along with their fair skin. "I guess that's true they do look like *mudder* and *dochder*."

"That's because they are, dumb-dumb."

She ignored her sister's rudeness. "April, I urge you to leave this alone. No good will come of it. Everyone respects Samuel and Mary. Samuel has just become a minister."

"Maybe I will and maybe I won't. He shouldn't have accepted the role of a minister. He's not fit for it. Come on, let's go into the *haus*. I'm starving. And you need to wash those hands before you eat."

"I always do."

"Where were you today?"

"Is that why you're back here because of the rumor? Because you wanted to spread it?"

"*Nee.* I had to get away from Philip, and I'm not sure I'll go back."

May gasped. It was unheard of for a young woman to leave her husband. May knew of two older couples who'd separated and lived apart, but April was so young and she'd never be allowed to marry again since divorce was forbidden. She had to make things work with Philip.

The twins were just about to walk through the doorway of their home when the rattling sounds of a wagon filled the air. April walked to the edge of the porch squinting. "Who's that?"

"Looks like it's Jeff Whiley."

April swung around and looked at May. "What does he want?"

"I don't know. Why don't you go inside and talk with *Mamm* while I see what he wants?"

"Nee, I'll come find out with you."

Jeff jumped down from his wagon. "Hello. Nice to see you girls again. I sure didn't expect to see you, April."

"Hello, Jeff. I'm on vacation, alone, before you ask if I brought Philip with me. What brings you here?" April asked.

"I've got a couple of boxes of food that someone paid for and didn't collect. They don't want it and it'll only go to waste. I thought your household might be able to use it. There are bananas and even some oranges."

"I love oranges," May said.

"Good to hear."

"Thanks so much, Jeff."

April narrowed her eyes at him. "Why bring food to us? We're not poor or anything."

"I'm just trying to do something nice for May. She's been looking a little down lately."

Swinging around, April looked at her twin. "Yeah, that's true. Well, *denke.* We surely appreciate it. Do you want to bring it into the kitchen?"

"Sure." Jeff put the two large boxes one atop the other and carried them toward the house while April talked with him. May followed along behind surprised at how strong Jeff was. He was slightly built, but he must've had a lot of muscle.

Their mother was delighted with the food and said it saved her a trip to the markets. "I must pay you for all this," she'd said, but Jeff wouldn't hear of it.

CHAPTER 9

THE NEXT DAY AT SCHOOL, May noticed Ivy and Grace got special treatment. She hadn't noticed if that had happened the previous day too, because May had spent most of the time listening to reading. For that reason, after May had done her two-hour duty, she left. She had to re-think her strategy regarding William. There was no point getting closer to William through his daughters if Deborah was also doing that.

As soon as she got home, April hurried over to the buggy. "Why don't we go somewhere today?"

April had been asleep when May left earlier. "I've been thinking a lot about what you said yesterday. How do you know about Mary and who told you?"

"I can't say."

"Why not? If you can't say, then maybe it's all lies that you made up."

"Let's just say, a little birdie told me."

May screwed up her face. "What does that even mean?"

"It means I'm not going to tell you, so stop asking. Why don't we pay Rebecca a visit? If anyone knows she'd know. I heard she was there when Lois was born. Right there in the room with both Beth and Mary."

"Huh? You said yesterday that Beth and Mary went away somewhere for the birth."

"Believe me, they did and Rebecca was there. Rebecca will tell you that too."

"And then if she tells you that Lois is definitely Beth's child, will you leave the matter alone?"

"She won't say that, but if she does, I'll never say anything about it again. I know Rebecca won't look me in the eye and tell me Lois is Beth's natural child."

May shook her head hoping she wouldn't be embarrassed by her twin, again. "Fine, get in."

"I'll just tell *Mamm* where we're going."

May climbed in the buggy and waited. Having April come home with news of that dreadful rumor, May was reminded what kind of a person her sister really was and that was one who liked causing trouble.

"You could be so embarrassed when you find out you're wrong," May said as April came back out of the house toward her.

April got in beside her. "You'll soon see when you find out the truth."

Nigel headed down the driveway as soon as May lifted the reins. "If it's true, you obviously can't say anything because if they wanted anyone to know about Lois they would've told people already."

April smiled at May. "Deep down, you know I'm right."

"I don't."

"I know the bishop doesn't like secrets and Rebecca is the bishop's *dochder,* so she'll have to do the right thing and tell us what she knows."

May stared at the road ahead. She was embarrassed at having to ask Rebecca such a thing and she knew it was causing trouble, but things might be worse if she didn't go with April.

When they arrived at Rebecca's house, April jumped down from the buggy. May got out and slipped the reins over the post and looked over just as Rebecca opened her front door. She watched as the girls embraced and then April was ushered inside. May then headed to the house and walked through to the kitchen to see April and Rebecca sitting at the kitchen table.

Rebecca jumped when she saw May. "May, I didn't know you were here too."

"I drove April here."

"I'm sorry for closing the door on you."

"The door was open."

"Was it?" Rebecca giggled. "Have a seat. Would you like a glass of iced tea?"

"*Jah* please."

Rebecca poured her a glass from the pitcher on the table. Then she pushed the glass toward May as she sat down.

April said, "As I was saying before May came in, I'm back because I'm having a vacation."

"Vacations are always good."

May looked around. "Where's Micah?"

"He's asleep."

"And how is married life working out for you, Rebecca?" April asked, smiling.

"It's going well, very well."

"Yes, mine too." April took a sip of iced tea. "The reason we're here today is that there's a rumor going around and we don't know whether it's true or not. We want you to clear things up for us."

"I said, I know it's not true," May said.

"What kind of a rumor?" Rebecca looked from one woman to the other.

"Someone told me that Mary is Lois's real mother and not Beth."

Rebecca shook her head and pushed her lips together. "Wherever would you have heard something like that?"

"I don't know, but that's what I've been told."

"Who started this? I must put a stop to it immediately."

April shook her head. "If there's no truth to it, it'll die down."

Rebecca shook her head. "Rumors like this can cause people a lot of grief. And there's a child involved."

"Rebecca, you're being upset over nothing unless

… unless it's true. Who delivered Lois? Were you the midwife? I heard you were there when Lois was born."

Rebecca bounded to her feet. "What's this really about, April?"

April pushed her chair back from the table. "You don't need to speak like that to me. I just want you to clear up the misunderstanding."

"I've never heard such a rumor. Tell me where it began and I will personally put a stop to it."

April hunched her shoulders. "Just say it's not true and then I'll tell the person who told me."

May saw that Rebecca was dreadfully upset and she didn't want Rebecca and April to go head-to-head in a heated argument. "Just tell her it's not true, Rebecca, and we'll leave."

Rebecca ignored her suggestion and glared at April. "April, you must tell me who said this."

April tilted her chin. "I don't have to do anything just because you tell me to."

Rebecca sat down and licked her lips. "Made-up stories like this can't carry on."

"And they wouldn't and won't if there's no truth to them. So, judging by your reaction, I think there is truth to it."

After Rebecca had folded her arms across her chest, she glared at April some more. "Are you trying to get back at Jacob? You told all those lies before you moved communities about Jacob being inappropriate with you. Are you upset everyone found out you were lying?"

May knew that was like waving a red flag at a bull. She jumped up. "Let's go, April."

April took a sip of tea acting as though she was as calm as anything. "You're not going to side-track me or upset me by mentioning a totally different issue. What you said just now is over with. If you'd told me I was wrong and that Lois was Beth's child, I would've believed you. And, I always tell the truth."

May knew that wasn't right and so did everyone else.

Rebecca stood up again. "I think you should leave now."

"So it is true?"

May put her hand under April's arm. "Come on, April, let's go."

"I don't think we should until Rebecca tells us the truth."

"I'm going." May walked to the kitchen door and came face to face with Anne, Rebecca's sister-in-law.

CHAPTER 10

"WHAT'S ALL the ruckus and raised voices? I heard you from next door."

April stood. "There's no problem. We were just leaving. We'll talk about this another time, Rebecca." She leaned down, and whispered, "I'm not letting this go."

"Come on, April." May then mouthed, 'I'm sorry' to Rebecca when April had walked past her. Once the twins were outside, May grabbed her sister's arm to make her stop walking. "What's gotten into you?"

"You're making a big deal out of nothing. Just get in the buggy and let's get out of here."

May folded her arms. "I don't want to get in the buggy with you. I don't want to be anywhere near you. What you did and said in there was just horrible."

"Please yourself. You can walk home then."

"Good. I will."

April jumped up in the buggy and trotted Nigel down the driveway. Nigel had betrayed her, May thought. He should've refused to move and then April might've been the one to walk home.

May blinked back tears as she strode down the driveway hoping Rebecca and Anne wouldn't see her and also praying they hadn't heard the spat she'd had with April.

May paced through the long grass by the side of the road hoping her mother would send April back to get her. Rebecca's reaction to everything had been odd and she could've said it wasn't true, but she didn't. May couldn't help but wonder if April might be right.

Could it possibly be true or partly true? Either way, it was none of her business and none of April's. She walked about a mile and had another five to go. She had her old black boots on and noticed a hole was forming near the little-toe side of the left one. At least they were more comfortable than her brand-new boots. Then she heard a buggy coming up behind her. Whoever they were, she hoped they'd give her a ride. When the buggy came close, she saw it was Jeff.

She stood still, and he stopped the buggy and leaned across. "What are you doing out here?"

"I had an argument with April and she left me to walk home."

"April's done that to you?"

"Unfortunately."

"Where are you heading?"

"Can you give me a ride? I'm just going home."

A smile softened his features. "Sure. Jump in."

She climbed up beside him. "Where are you off to?"

"Home for the midday meal. I do that every day."

"That seems silly. Why don't you eat at the markets?"

"*Mamm* likes me to come home. I think she gets lonely at home all day long by herself. And it gives me a real break in my workday."

"I'm glad you came along when you did. It seems no one was coming to get me."

"I thought you and April got along well. She is your twin after all."

"*Jah*, well, she forgets that sometimes."

He glanced over at her. "That's sad. I always wanted to have a twin when I was growing up because all my brothers and sisters were so much older. There was never anyone for me to play with unless I had a friend over. I used to daydream of having a twin or at least a brother close in age, so we could do things together. It's no good being by yourself all the time when you're a kid."

"I suppose that's true. There were good times when we were young, but when she does strange things it reflects onto me. Everyone sees us as the same person. I have no identity of my own. We're known as 'the twins.' I'm lumped together with her."

"How long's she staying?"

May shook her head. "She hasn't said."

"You know where to find me if you want someone to speak with. I'm a good listener and I've been known to give good advice."

"*Denke*, Jeff."

He pulled into the driveway. "Here you are."

May couldn't see Nigel or the buggy anywhere. "Looks as though April's still out somewhere. She would've left the buggy for me to unhitch."

"Do you want me to take you someplace else? Or take you to find her?"

"It's okay. She could be anywhere. *Denke* for the ride." She jumped down from the buggy. "I'll see you later."

"Sooner than later, I hope."

"Maybe. Bye, Jeff." She hurried into the house and heard him call out an answering goodbye. When she found her mother in the kitchen, she had to tell her that she and April had gotten into an argument. She didn't want to tell her what it was about, but her mother got it out of her.

"That's a dreadful thing for her to say about Mary. It's ridiculous; just forget about it. April's stirring up trouble again. Just forget about it for the moment. I'll talk to her when she gets home."

"I'm worried she's making things worse right now. I mean, where is she?"

Her mother pressed her lips together tightly. "We have to hope and pray she's not spreading the rumor.

All we can do is pray about it and leave it in *Gott's* hands."

There she was again with her solution for every-thing — *pray about it.* "You're right. I'm going to do my best to forget about it until she gets home, or I'll get too stressed."

"Good idea."

May kept herself busy for the rest of the day by doing chores, and she did take her *Mamm's* advice by sending up prayers as she worked. April didn't come back until four o'clock that afternoon. May went out to see that her sister hadn't driven Nigel too hard. After she saw he was okay, she started slowly unhitching him before turning her full attention to April. "Where have you been?"

"I had a little talk with the bishop."

She stared at April hoping she wasn't serious, but by the smug look on her face, May guessed it was true. "It didn't work out so well the last time you talked to the bishop about something."

"As I said to Rebecca, that's in the past. I don't know why everybody keeps talking about it. In my commu-nity, people forget the past and move forward."

"Very convenient," May said wryly. "You really talked to the bishop about that ridiculous rumor?"

"I did — and he didn't think it was ridiculous."

"I can't see why he would think any of it was true."

"As a simple way to clear it up, he's calling a meeting of all the oversight to discuss it."

"Is that so?"

April smiled at her. "It is. And what's more, he's having Rebecca there too."

"Why didn't you just leave things be?"

"Because why keep something like that a secret?"

"You're gonna look so foolish if it's not true."

"I think it is true and even more so after talking to Rebecca."

May shook her head, disturbed that the bishop had listened to her sister. "Don't be silly."

April stepped forward. "Rebecca could've cleared it up by telling us which woman gave birth to Lois, but she didn't." When the phone in the barn rang out, they both raced to answer it. By elbowing May out of the way, April got there first. "Hello. Oh, hi. *Jah,* she's here." She looked over at April, and covered the receiver with her hand, and whispered, "It's for you; it's William."

May couldn't believe it. With her heart pumping hard, she grabbed the receiver. "Hello?"

"Hello, May, this is Sarah Miller from the school board."

May glared at April who sniggered. Then she hoped she hadn't done something wrong at school. "Hello, Sarah."

"Deborah called to say she wasn't feeling well today and she'll be taking tomorrow off. We're wondering if you might be able to fill in for her?"

She was immediately relieved. "For the whole day tomorrow?"

"*Jah,* the whole day."

"I would love to, *jah.*"

Sarah said, "I'll bring the schoolhouse keys to your *haus* tonight"

"Okay. What's wrong with Deborah?"

"It seems she's caught some kind of a virus."

"I hope she'll be okay."

"These things sometimes only last a day or two. I'll see you soon."

"Okay, bye." She hung up and looked at April.

April cackled. "I got you good. What did she want?"

May shook her head at April, who still thought she was hilariously funny for telling May it was William on the phone.

"What's going on?" April asked again.

"Deborah's sick and I'm filling in for her at school tomorrow."

April's face soured. "What made you want to do that?"

"You know I've been helping out there."

"I know that, but you never told me why."

"Because I like to help children."

April threw her head back and laughed. "You already told me why you're going there. The only person you want to help is yourself. It's all about William Bronstein."

"April, that isn't a good thing to say."

"I can't help it if it's true."

May sighed. Just because April was devious didn't

mean she had to act like her. "Okay, I guess you're right. Someone suggested I get a job at the school because William's *kinner* go there and it's a way of getting closer to them and to him."

April rolled her eyes. "That will take you forever and meanwhile someone else can snap him up. Does he know you like him at least?"

"Nee. I've never really spoken to him."

April shook her head. "How do you know you like him?"

"Because ... by watching him, and he seems really nice. I like the look of him."

"He's a lot older than you."

"So is your husband."

"Only by two years and that's nothing."

May sighed as she started unhitching the buggy. "I didn't know any other way to get to know him."

"What about the barn raising? I heard there's one soon."

"Ach nee, that's tomorrow. I think Deborah likes him too. I hope she doesn't show up there if she's not well enough to go to school. I was looking forward to going to the barn raising. I was going to head there after my two hours at school tomorrow."

"She's ruined things there for you, hasn't she? She's blocked your chances. Does she know you like him?"

"Nee, she couldn't possibly know."

"Are you sure?"

"Quite sure."

"Just how many people have you flapped your gums to?"

May screwed up her face.

"How many people have you told?" April asked through gritted teeth.

May didn't know why April was acting so angry. Her moods seemed worse since she'd gotten married. "Not that many. Only two people know."

"I hope things go well, but I doubt they will. Deborah sounds like she's moving in fast." April yawned loudly. "I think I'll have a little rest before the evening meal."

"Aren't you going to help us prepare it?"

"Nee, dumb heita. Why should I? I'm on vacation. I don't live here anymore, remember? I'm here for a well-earned rest." April stomped away and May was hurt at being called a dumb head.

A long time ago, May had learned the best way to handle April was to keep out of her way. She continued to unhitch Nigel from the buggy, trying to let April's unkind words have no effect on her.

CHAPTER 11

WHEN MAY WALKED into the kitchen, her mother and April were in a heated discussion over April telling the bishop lies about Mary.

Her mother looked up at May. "Do you know what's going on? She's stirred up trouble with the bishop."

"I know. She told me." May sat at the table with them.

"The facts are the facts. I just don't know the smaller details of how it all played out."

Their mother said, "Go on, tell me everything from start to finish. And I will have to tell your *vadder.*"

"It doesn't bother me," April said. "I've done nothing wrong."

"And neither have I," May was quick to point out, since she usually got the blame for whatever April did.

April proceeded to tell her mother everything she'd told the bishop.

Her mother stared at her in horror. "You mean you said all that to the bishop?"

"Yeah, I did."

"Who would've told you a dreadful thing like that?"

"It's all true, *Mamm*," April assured her. "And I have to go to the bishop's place tonight for the meeting."

Mamm gasped. "You're being called to a meeting of the oversight?"

"I am."

"Then you'll probably be shunned and you won't be shunned under this roof. You'll go back to Philip's community and that community will learn everything." Their mother shook her head. "This is awful, just awful."

April screwed up her nose. "You've got it all wrong, *Mamm*, because it's true. Everything I said is true."

"But you're talking about Samuel, a man who is beyond reproach, almost."

"Well that's not so and everybody will find out he's kept a lie going."

"Your *vadder* will drive you to Bishop Elmer's tonight. This better not be something you've made up like last time. If you're fibbing again, our reputation will be ruined."

"Don't worry, *Mamm*, your reputation is quite safe because I know what I'm talking about. It's true and soon everybody will know and the bishop will be thanking me. That'll make up for the mistake I made last time. Just you wait and see."

May shook her head. Unable to keep quiet, she blurted out, "I think it's dreadful what you're doing and even if it's true, so what? People have the right to live their lives as they see fit."

"*Mamm,* this secret must come out. I'm glad you agree with me."

Mamm shook her head at April. "I certainly hope you're wrong, but either way it's going to be very dreadful for you and for us. I'm serious about you going back home."

"Of course I will. I intend to go back. I'm only here for a vacation, a little break."

May stared at April wondering why she would need a break from her husband since they'd only been married a short time. Their marriage had been a hasty one and maybe she regretted it, as she'd more or less said before.

"There's another thing that confirms what I heard," April said to her mother.

"What is it?"

"May and I went to visit Rebecca, who was there when Lois was born and she didn't deny it."

Her mother drew back from the table and looked at May. "Is that so?"

"Well, she didn't say it was true and she didn't say it wasn't. The only reason she didn't deny it was that she was horrified April could make up such a fantastical story."

Their mother looked at April. "I wish you wouldn't involve yourself with things like this. You should leave things well enough alone. I hope this doesn't blow up in your face like the last time."

"Don't worry, *Mamm*. I know what I'm doing. The bishop will thank me, you'll see."

"Is this your way for making up for last time?" May asked.

April glared at her. "You don't have to be mean."

"I was just asking."

CHAPTER 12

THE TWINS' mother had an early dinner ready so they could eat as soon as their father arrived home. When they heard his buggy, *Mamm* slipped outside to tell him about the meeting at the bishop's.

April and May placed the prepared casserole and vegetables on the table and stared out the window. In the failing light of the afternoon sun, they saw their father's stressed face as he was being told the news.

"He's not happy," May said.

"It's not my fault. I could drive myself. *Mamm's* just making a big deal out of everything."

"They do their best to keep out of people's personal dramas and quarrels and you've put them right in the middle."

April stepped away from the window. "Not deliberately. It's not my fault."

Biting on her tongue, May remained silent. Then April pulled on May's sleeve.

"He's coming inside. I should've spoken to *Dat* first. *Mamm* would've made it sound bad."

Both April and May sat at the table waiting for their parents to enter the kitchen.

Their father appeared and stood in the doorway like a looming presence, with his wife beside him. "What have you done now, April?"

"It's all true and the bishop will thank me when he finds out that secrets were being kept. I know Bishop Elmer doesn't like secrets."

"Sit down, Simon," their mother said as she gently moved her husband forward.

Once they were all seated and had said their prayer for the food, there was silence. May knew her father was not looking forward to going out at night after a hard day's work. And the worst thing of all for him was to go to the bishop's place and for one of his daughters to be one of Samuel's accusers.

"Let me state this here and now." Everybody looked up at May. "This has nothing to do with me. April is acting separately and on her own. Just because I'm April's twin doesn't mean I agree with everything she does."

"May, we don't need you to add this extra stress on everything," said *Mamm*. "You always overreact to everything. No one said this had anything to do with you. You're not the one going to the bishop's *haus* for the meeting, April is. Now, can we stop talking about it? I feel a headache coming on."

Their father sympathetically rubbed their mother's back.

The silence continued until dinner was over and April and their father were out the door. May and her mother cleared the table. *Mamm* breathed out heavily. "I do hope everything will be alright."

"Me too, but you never know what will happen."

Mamm placed the dishes down in the sink and stared at May. "Exactly what did Rebecca say when April confronted her?"

"She was upset. I guess because it was so unexpected."

"But she didn't deny it?"

"Nee, she didn't. And I wish she had done so, because I don't know now. Part of me thinks there might be some truth to it because of Rebecca's reaction."

"Oh dear." *Mamm* shook her head. "If it's true it will be dreadful for us."

"Why do you say that?"

"People will view us as the troublemakers and avoid us."

"April is the one who is doing it."

"And it reflects badly on us. Anything she does looks bad for us. There's what she said about Jacob last time."

May nodded. *"Jah,* that was dreadful. But people don't blame us for that."

"Only because not everyone found out about it. If this is true, everyone will find out and then everyone will know. And the other reason why people didn't find out about Jacob was because April left to stay with my sister for a while."

May cast her mind back to the day April left. She hadn't wanted to go, but she hadn't wanted to face the fruits of her false accusation. *Mamm* finally talked her into going just for a few weeks and when she got there she met Philip. Philip and she had gotten married quite quickly.

Mamm filled the sink with hot sudsy water, then switched off the faucet. "All we can do is wait and see what happens tonight."

CHAPTER 13

REBECCA WAS full of nerves as she traveled to her parents' house. She'd answered the phone in the barn just a few hours ago and was surprised it was her father. He told her she needed to be at this meeting. All he'd said was that accusations had been made toward Samuel and Mary regarding Lois. Rebecca had no idea how anybody had found out. She hoped that Samuel and Mary didn't think she was the one who had said anything.

When she stopped by the front of the house, she was surprised to see April getting out of a buggy. April must be the instigator of this. Perhaps it was a coincidence ... but Rebecca knew that couldn't be the case — not after the way April had talked earlier when she and May had stopped in to 'visit' her.

April glanced over at her and then ushered inside by April's father, Simon.

Just as Rebecca was securing her horse, she heard another buggy. It was Samuel's buggy. She waited for them to approach. Mary got out and hurried to Rebecca. "Do you know what this is all about?"

"All I know is that someone is accusing you of covering up Lois's identity. That's what I was told and I don't know any more than that."

Mary stood on tiptoes and looked at the other buggy. "Who else is here?"

"Simon and April."

"They wouldn't know anything," Mary said, just as Samuel joined them.

"I know, that's what I thought."

"We should go in," Samuel said.

The three of them walked into the bishop's house. When they got to the living room Rebecca faced a group of old men sitting around in a circle. These old men including her father made up the church over-sight. Before she sat down in one of the three remaining chairs, she glanced over at Mary and Samuel feeling sorry for them. On the other side of the circle was April and her father. April was looking very serious and Rebecca hoped April had not gone about things this way. If April truly had found out about Lois, the proper thing would've been to go to Samuel and Mary and talk with them. Of course, Rebecca guessed her father, being the bishop, might have a different opinion.

Rebecca knew *Mamm* would be in the kitchen

listening to what was happening and her younger brothers would've been banished to their rooms for an early night.

The bishop stood and, after clearing his throat, started with, "We're gathered here tonight because there has been a surprising story that we've heard from May."

"I'm April." April stood up.

"I'm sorry. From April."

April nodded and then sat down. Rebecca could feel the tension in the room and she just wanted to run away.

The bishop continued, "April, we all know by now that you've said that Lois is really Mary's child. Firstly, can you tell us where you heard such a thing against Mary and Samuel?"

Samuel bounded to his feet. "There's no need to go any further. It's true. I don't know how April found out, but Mary and I thought it best to leave things be after Beth died."

The bishop was visibly stunned as he stood there with his mouth opened. "It's true?"

"It is. Mary and I have talked about this extensively and we were going to tell Lois when she was older, but she already knows Mary as her mother and … we weren't really sure what to do."

Mary stood. "That's right, so we ended up doing nothing up until now."

The bishop shook his head. "Why didn't you come to me with this Samuel?"

Rebecca looked down at the floorboards and blocked everything else out. She didn't even look at April, but she could feel Mary and Samuel's pain.

MAY COULDN'T WAIT for April to get home, so she could hear what had happened at the meeting. The bishop would've got to the bottom of things and he would know the truth by now one way or another. She glanced at the clock to see fifteen minutes past ten. Surely April and *Dat* would be coming home soon.

"Good, May, you're awake too." Her mother walked into the living room and sat down with her.

"I couldn't sleep until she came home." May put aside the sampler she was working on.

"Me either. I tried to sleep but I'm too curious to find out what happened. I need to know if our family name is ruined — again."

When they heard the buggy, the two women rushed to the door. *Mamm* got there first to open it. April jumped down from the buggy and hurried to the door leaving her father to unhitch the buggy. "Samuel admitted it," she said.

May and her mother clung to each other in shock. "Exactly what did he say?" their mother asked.

"He admitted to the deception."

May was sick to her stomach and sorry for Samuel and Mary.

April pushed her way through the door. "At first, the bishop said I had to tell them who told me such a dreadful thing and then Samuel stood up and confessed it all. It was just as I said. I told you I was right."

May looked over at her mother to see her hands trembling as they covered her mouth. "What happens now?" May turned back to April.

"Samuel is no longer a minister. He's been demoted."

"Because of you?" May asked.

"*Nee*, because of his lies. Nothing to do with me. The truth would've come out eventually anyway."

Her mother stood there staring with her mouth open and May couldn't take it any longer. "I'm going to bed." May stomped up the stairs and closed the door and hoped her sister wouldn't come in to talk to her anymore tonight. She hated that April had been right.

MAY WOKE the next morning to the sounds of someone in the kitchen. Then she heard a buggy horse trotting away from the house and knew her father was leaving. Flinging the covers off, she was glad April had left her alone the night before.

May ate a quiet breakfast alone since her mother and April were still in bed, and then she headed to school early. It was good to have a whole day at school because she needed to keep her mind off the problem April had uncovered. An hour after she arrived at school the first of the children arrived.

She moved out into the warm morning sun to greet the children, who were being brought there by their parents. She overheard two of those parents talking about Samuel and Mary. It seemed everybody knew. It never took long for information to travel the communication highway in their close-knit community.

Deborah had left May instructions for the day, so she knew what work needed to be done by the children of different ages.

When the school day drew to a close, May was exhausted but pleased. The day had gone smoothly. She waited outside until all the children were gone and was upset to see that Ivy and Grace were collected by William's sister, Nancy. That had to mean that William was still at the barn raising.

As she headed home, the events of the last few days whirled in her head. It was too much. When she spotted Aunt Agatha's house, she decided to stop in and see how she was. She wasn't ready to face April right now.

Aunt Agatha was the bishop's aunt and everyone in the community called her Aunt Agatha whether they were related or not. When the old lady opened the door, a smile spread across her face at the sight of May. "What a nice surprise. Do come in."

"*Denke.* I just wanted to say hello to see how you're doing."

"Let's sit by the fire."

"Okay." May followed Aunt Agatha through to the living room. Two cats were spread out asleep on the rug by the hearth and another was asleep on one of the chairs.

Aunt Agatha sat on the couch and May sat beside her. "What's troubling you, May?"

"Oh, is it so obvious?"

"*Jah.*"

"I'm a little upset because … I suppose April might be right and a minister who's holding such a secret probably shouldn't be a minister, but who was he hurting? I didn't see how the secret was upsetting to anybody else. And maybe they were only keeping it quiet out of respect for Beth."

"I wholeheartedly agree with you, May." Aunt Agatha slowly nodded. "It's a heart-wrenching thing when there's a child involved. It would've been a hard decision for Mary to make back then, to give away her *boppli.* She would've done it with others' best interests in mind, I know that."

"I know it, too."

"Can I get you hot tea?"

"*Nee,* I'm fine, *denke.*"

"How's April?"

"She's here on vacation, she says."

Aunt Agatha's thin lips turned down at the corners. "She only just got married."

"I know."

"You're not getting on with your twin?"

May sighed. "How do you know?"

"Because you'd be talking with her and not me."

"I see. It's hard to get along with her sometimes. She brought trouble with her. She left amidst trouble and then she brings it back with her."

Aunt Agatha nodded.

"I suppose you know the trouble she caused about Jacob?" May stared at Aunt Agatha, hoping she wasn't upsetting her with all this talk.

"I do. I hear everything that happens."

"I'm sorry to say it, but I wish April had never come back."

"Is that so?"

May nodded. *"Jah."*

"Well, leave it to me."

May was taken aback. "What are you going to do?"

"Something."

"Really?"

Aunt Agatha's mouth twitched at the corners.

"What are you going to do?"

"Never you mind."

May gave a little laugh and she felt better for talking with Aunt Agatha. "I just might have that cup of tea, if you have the time?"

"*Jah*, come into the kitchen. I had just boiled the kettle before you arrived."

May followed Aunt Agatha into the kitchen and behind her walked two of the cats. It seemed they were following Aunt Agatha. May sat and had tea with Aunt Agatha, but the elderly woman never told May what she had planned.

CHAPTER 14

WHEN MAY GOT HOME, she rushed to find April, who was sitting in the kitchen shelling peas for dinner. "What happened at the barn raising? Was Deborah there?" May sat down at the table.

April's lips pressed firmly together. "She came there around three o'clock."

"I knew it. I just had a feeling she'd do that. She probably wasn't sick at all." May reached forward and grabbed a few peas and popped them into her mouth.

"More than likely." April nodded. "Because she spent a good part of the time talking with William, who'd finished his shift by then."

"Who told you about Lois?"

April licked her lips. "Well, it was the midwife, indirectly. She was Marilyn's cousin. Rebecca was only a trainee midwife at the time and was getting experience working with her. Anyway, I'm good friends with a woman who's the other cousin."

May held her head. "It's so confusing."

"Not at all. The midwife who was at Lois's birth has two cousins. One of them is Marilyn, our community midwife, and her other cousin is my friend."

"Wasn't the midwife sworn to secrecy?" May asked.

"If she was, she didn't take notice. I don't think she thought it would ever get back if she told her cousin."

"Hmm, I suppose she wouldn't have known it would get back to someone who knew Mary. Did she name names?"

"*Nee* she didn't. But I recognized all the people by the story she told."

May sighed. "I feel so sorry for Mary, and Samuel."

"Well, good for you. Will you make me a cup of hot tea?"

May bounded to her feet. "Can you tell me more about the barn raising?"

"There's nothing to report. It was just a regular barn raising."

May filled the teakettle with water, and once she had set it on the gas stovetop, she sat down again with April hoping to learn more. "Tell me about William's reaction to Deborah. Did he seem like he liked her?"

"It was pretty hard to tell. He was smiling a lot though."

May shook her head. "That's something I didn't want to hear."

"Do you want me to lie to you?"

"It's okay. I have to go to school early again tomorrow morning because I have the keys to the school room."

"That was so selfish of her to have a day off for nothing," April said.

"She could have really been sick. Although, she can't have been *that* sick if she ended up there today."

April leaned across her, and whispered, "Is *Mamm* really angry with me? She just went straight to bed without barely saying two words to me."

"She's worried about what people will think of us now."

"They'll be pleased that I called attention to the lie that's been going on for years."

May shook her head. "I don't know about that. I think she might be right."

"We'll soon see. We'll find out on Sunday."

After she had jumped up to turn off the kettle, May asked, "What happens on Sunday?"

"Oh, didn't I tell you?"

"*Nee?*"

"Samuel and Mary have to make a confession in front of everybody at the meeting."

May gasped. "Really?"

"*Jah,* I'm not making it up."

May stood when she remembered she'd been going to make the tea. While she placed the tea leaves in the pot, April was still trying to justify what she'd done. "It just gets worse." May placed the teapot down in front of April and then sat with her.

"It's not my fault," April stood to get the teacups and saucers from the cupboard.

"They're going to be so embarrassed."

"Can't you see that it's better this way? I don't know what your problem is."

May jumped to her feet. "I should get an early night because I've got to wake up early for school."

"Wait. Aren't you going to have tea with me?"

"Nee. All of a sudden, I've grown very tired. *Gut nacht."*

"But, who's going to make the dinner for *Dat?"*

"You will." May hurried away without waiting for April's response.

THE NEXT DAY, May got to school well before Deborah and started marking the papers that she hadn't gotten around to from the day before. Working at the school had been good for her, keeping her mind off April.

The morning went well, with May helping Deborah as usual. May left around lunchtime and headed home. Friday afternoon was when they normally went to the store and May had left a note for her mother to wait for her.

May headed into the house. *"Mamm,* are you ready?" April came running out to her, grabbed her arm and pulled her back out onto the porch. "Stop it. What are you doing?"

"Philip's here."

"He's here?"

"*Jah.* He's come to take me back with him."

May smiled. "That's so sweet. He's missing you."

"*Nee*, he's not. Aunt Agatha told his mother he should fetch me and then she said I was causing trouble here."

May gulped and hoped April didn't know she was the one who had talked to Aunt Agatha about her. "You had to go home sooner or later."

April wiped away a tear. "I'm just not ready to go now. Philip's insisting I go back tomorrow. I won't even get to hear what Samuel and Mary say on Sunday."

"That's an awful thing to say. Why would you be pleased about wanting to see them have to make their confession in front of everyone? It's like you're taking delight in their sorrow."

"I just want to see it through. That's all."

"I'll write to you and tell you about it. When are you leaving?"

"Tomorrow morning. This is just awful. I've been talking to *Mamm* all day and she's still upset with me. I thought she would've seen things my way."

"Everyone's got their own opinions about things."

April tugged on her sleeve again. "We should go inside. They'll think we're talking about them."

"We are."

The twins giggled as they walked back inside. May was determined to put their differences aside and make the most of her time left with April. That was lots easier to do knowing April was going back home in the morning.

CHAPTER 15

EARLY THE NEXT morning May stood beside her parents as they waved goodbye to Philip and April riding off in a taxi to the train station. Philip was perfectly lovely and May didn't see why April had been so reluctant to go home. He genuinely didn't seem to notice April's flaws.

Since they hadn't gotten to the markets the previous day, May shopped with her mother that morning and then spent the rest of the day baking. May wanted to reach out to Mary and tell her how sorry she was about everything, but she knew her mother would not approve of her sticking her nose into things. Her mother's opinion was always to keep out of situations.

SUNDAY CAME TOO QUICKLY for May. After the

preaching was through, the bishop said that Samuel and Mary had a confession to make. May's heartbeat quickened as she watched the couple walk to the front of the room.

With Mary by his side, Samuel made his confession that Lois was not Beth's child and he had only found that out after his sister's death when Mary came to care for Lois as her nursemaid.

May looked around the sea of faces. Nobody seemed shocked because everybody already knew, but nevertheless, Samuel had to make his confession and apologize to the community on behalf of himself and Mary.

Mary stood there with her arms down by her side looking glum. Lois was in one of the bedrooms with the other younger children who were being looked after by a couple of the older ladies. May was glad Lois couldn't hear what was said.

At least now Lois would grow up knowing the truth that Mary was her real mother and Beth had looked after her for a short period of time.

"Would you like to say something, Mary?" the bishop asked.

Mary looked up. *"Jah."* She stepped forward and told her story and the reason she had given Lois over to Beth.

May wiped away a tear and when she looked up, she saw she wasn't the only one crying.

"Denke." The bishop then said a few words to

118

smooth things over and then he announced that Samuel would no longer be acting as a minister.

May knew that both Samuel and Mary were suffering. Their lives would never be the same with that deception story hanging over them. On the upside, April had freed them and Lois from the burden of carrying the deception, and that must've given Samuel and Mary a little comfort.

When the meeting was over, May walked out of the house wanting to talk to Mary and tell her how sorry she was that this had all come out. Mary was surrounded by a crowd of women who seemed sympathetic, so May had to leave that talk for another time.

William's girls ran over to May. "When are you coming back to school, Miss May?"

"Monday, I'd say. I'll have to check with Miss Deborah. You could see me back there tomorrow or maybe the week after depending—"

"Come and talk to *Dat*." The girls took hold of her arm and led her to William.

She couldn't keep the smile from her face because the plan to get to William through his girls had worked. When she got closer, he looked at her and then folded his arms across his chest. He then shushed the girls who were talking to him.

"Girls, leave us."

"But, *Dat* ..."

"Ivy, I said leave."

The two girls looked at one another and then did as he ordered.

"Have I done something wrong?" May asked.

"I hear you were responsible for what just happened here today."

"What's that?" May asked, scarcely believing her ears.

"If you knew something about Samuel you should've gone to him directly and not gone to the bishop first."

"I totally agree, but it wasn't me. It was April. I had nothing to do with it."

He scratched the back of his neck. "Well, if she knew about it, surely you knew about it."

"*Jah,* but it wasn't my place to say anything. She told me about it and I didn't want her to make trouble."

"You should've gone to Samuel and Mary. The way this has happened is not right."

"I totally agree, but I can't be held responsible for my —"

"You *are* responsible. Did you hear what I said?"

She stared at him, shocked that he was blaming her and judging her.

"So if I hear gossip, I'm supposed to go to the person gossiped about? *Nee,* I will not. I will keep out of it and not spread it further."

"I think you and I do things a little differently. I don't think you should be looking after the children in school. I'll talk to Deborah about that."

"Don't bother — if you have that attitude, I won't go back and I'll talk to Deborah myself." She walked away from him and to the other end of the yard behind a crowd of people. Then she felt a hand on her shoulder and turned around. It was her mother.

"What's upset you?"

"Just a *vadder* of some of the school children. He said something horrible. He's blaming me because I knew about Samuel and Mary and I didn't say anything, but I didn't know it was true."

"Don't worry, I think you did the right thing."

"Do you? Do you really?"

Her mother nodded. "I do. Don't worry about the nasty things people say."

"He didn't want me working at the school so I don't want to go back. I will never work there again."

"You can't let him stop you. That's ridiculous. Who said that to you?"

She shook her head as she fought back tears. She had enjoyed working with the children. "I'd rather do something where there are no barriers. I'll get a proper job—a paid one."

"Of course you should if that's what you want."

Jeff was nearby and joined the conversation. "Looking for a job, May?"

"I am."

"My *vadder's* looking for someone a few hours a day."

Her mother smiled at her. "Excuse me."

When her mother left, May said, *"Denke,* but I'm not sure what I want to do and the next decision I make must be the right decision."

"Fair enough. The offer's there. I will personally recommend you and *Dat* will give you the job on my say-so."

"Denke, Jeff. You've been very kind."

"I saw you talking to William. It looked like he had a problem with you. He was upset over something."

"I don't think so."

"He seemed upset."

She shrugged. "It had something to do with Samuel being embarrassed. He thought I should've said something to Samuel rather than keep quiet about what April found out."

"Do you want me to talk to him? Because I will."

She smiled at the image of the slightly-built Jeff, speaking to William, who towered over him. "It's okay. I appreciate it, but it's fine."

"Where's April?"

"She's gone back with her husband. He came for her and they left yesterday."

"Oh, that was a quick visit."

"It was. She came, caused a huge problem, and then left."

"Perhaps it was all for the best that it came out."

She nodded. "I think you're right. Sometimes things happen for the best."

"All things work together for good," he said, quoting a partial scripture.

ON THE RIDE home from the meeting, May noticed her mother's attitude toward her had changed completely. She'd been ignored while *Mamm* complained to *Dat* about what people had said about Samuel and Mary.

"You can't worry about what people say," *Dat* said.

"Well, I do. Everyone turned aside and no one wanted to speak with me."

"It's not my fault," May said from the backseat of the buggy.

"No one said anything about that," her father said.

"They did to me, and even with those people who didn't say it, I could sense tension. It's all right for April. She leaves and then I get all the blame for the whole thing. I had nothing to do with it."

Her mother turned around. "It might as well be your fault. You could've put a stop to it. You've got the influence over April and you could've told her to stop, or told Samuel at least."

May gasped at her mother's sudden change of heart. She knew she had no influence over April whatsoever. "Well, if I'd gone to Samuel I would've looked like the big trouble-making gossiper. That's not who I am."

"Our name is ruined. I feel so ashamed." Her mother sobbed loudly with her hand covering her mouth.

"It's not my fault. Stop it, *Mamm.* There's no need to cry over it. Stop!"

"Don't talk to your *mudder* like that, May."

"Well, why's she blaming me?"

"Go to your room as soon as we get home," *Mamm* said between sobs.

"Why?" May yelled.

Her mother looked at her father and May knew she was in big trouble. No one said anything more and the remainder of the drive home was spent in silence.

May got out of the buggy and headed to the house in front of her mother. She opened the front door and then went directly to her room. After she lay down on her bed for a while, thinking how awful her life was, she got up and looked out the window. It was unbelievable. April had conveniently left, and now she was the one taking all the blame. She'd warned April it wasn't a good idea to keep talking about it.

May looked down at the ground below and wondered if she should slip out the window. She could step onto one of the branches of the tree that was next to the house, and then make her way down to the ground. If she was younger, she'd run away from home. It was only mid-afternoon and she had no idea how long she'd be banished to her room.

Just after six that evening, a knock sounded on her door. "Come in." May waited but nobody opened the door and then she heard footsteps leaving.

She opened her door to see a tray on the floor. It

held a bowl of the soup she and her mother had made the previous day, along with two crusts of bread. That meant she was still in trouble, but at least they'd brought her food. She took the tray into her room, set it on her bed and prayed. Then she dipped the bread into the soup. The bread wasn't yesterday's, it was so stiff it must've been bread from several days ago. Normally, *Mamm* would've made breadcrumbs out of such old bread and that showed May that *Mamm* was still angry with her.

Why was she in trouble? It was so unfair. When she finished yesterday's soup and the stale bread, she placed the tray outside her door not knowing if it was safe to venture out. She hadn't been given permission yet, so May got into bed and pulled the covers over her head.

The next thing May knew, it was morning and the sun was spreading its warm glow over the horizon. She pulled on her dressing gown, crept down the stairs and then looked about. There was a used pan in the sink and that meant her father had left for work and her mother had gone back to bed. Then she heard the stairs creaking, so she walked out of the kitchen knowing it was her mother. Her mother was fully-dressed and wore a stern expression. "Are you still mad with me, *Mamm?*"

"I am and so is your *vadder.*"

"Where is *Dat?*"

"He had to leave early for work."

"And why did you send me to my room?"

"I'm not happy about your actions. I'm very disappointed in both you girls. You're a shame to my family. I wish you'd never been born."

May was shocked at her mother. "Surely, you can't mean that?"

"I do."

"You wish I'd never been born? Like, you'd never ever had me and then you would never have had *kinner?*"

Her mother turned away. "I'll get myself breakfast when you leave." She turned and walked back up the stairs.

An escape from this house was what she needed. She had nowhere to go. April was having problems with Philip, so she couldn't even go visit them for a few weeks. And, she couldn't escape to the school today because … wait … she remembered that she hadn't spoken to Deborah like she'd told William she would. Deborah was still expecting her at the school. Just because William had said she shouldn't be teaching the children didn't mean she was no longer welcome. That was Deborah's decision to make, unless other parents complained.

CHAPTER 16

MAY ATE a quick breakfast and then drove herself to the school feeling awful because her father was also upset with her. She arrived at school just after seven thirty and was relieved to see Deborah's horse and buggy already there. She patted Nigel on his neck before she left him. "At least you're still talking to me. You are, aren't you?" He didn't pull away or shake his head, so she assumed Nigel was still her best horsey friend.

When she walked into the school room, Deborah was surprised. "What are you doing here so early?"

"I couldn't sleep last night, so I thought I'd come early and help."

"*Denke.* There's so much you can do. I'm marking some more papers. Can you help with that?"

"I'd love to." May threw herself into the schoolwork and stayed in the room when the children arrived hoping William wouldn't find out she was there. She heaved a sigh of relief when the school day started and there wasn't a parent in sight.

By lunchtime, she could no longer chase away the torment whirling in her mind. She'd tried her best to concentrate on the children, but she was too upset over how her parents had treated her.

May needed time by herself to think things through before she faced her parents again. There were only a handful of people she could count on to be nice to her, but the only person she wanted to confide in right now was Jeff. Remembering he went home every day for the midday meal, she went in the direction of his place hoping to bump into him along the way. When she was nearly at his house, she saw him coming at her from the opposite direction. She continued on and they met in the middle of the quiet road.

"Hello, May. Aren't you at the school today?"

"*Jah*, I was but I've finished for today. Do you have a minute to talk?"

"Of course. Do you want to come home with me and we can talk over food? We've always got plenty."

She glanced back at his house. "*Nee*, this is something I wouldn't want your mother to hear."

"Let's get our buggies off the road then."

She went up the road a little where she could get Nigel and the buggy safely off the road. Just as she jumped down, Jeff came hurrying to her.

"What is it?" He stood still with his hands resting on his hips.

She blew out a deep breath. "Everyone's blaming me for what April did. The thing with revealing Samuel and Mary's big secret."

"Nee they're not."

"They are. William said something to me, and my parents … well, I had a big argument with *Mamm* and ended up spending the whole time in my room when I got home yesterday."

"Ah, that's not good. You said you've been to school?"

"Jah."

"And Deborah was okay with you?"

She frowned wondering what he'd heard. Maybe she'd said something to him and didn't remember. *"Jah,* but I don't know for how long if William talks to her. He said he doesn't want me around the children."

"The bishop should know about that. It's not fair."

May shook her head. "It was the bishop who started this whole thing. Except, it wasn't even me who did it."

"People will forget in time."

"It's just not fair." May shook her head and looked down at the dirt underneath her feet.

"Things like this never are. Won't you have something to eat with me? Say hello to my *mudder?"*

"Nee. Denke, but I'm in no mood to talk with anyone. Especially someone as nice as her. I'm just too grumpy."

"What can I do to help?"

May shook her head. "I don't know. I just wish I didn't get the blame for the things April does."

"How about I take you somewhere for lunch and we can talk some more?"

May remembered him saying his mother liked him to come home in the middle of the day because she got lonely. "I shouldn't hold you up any longer. *Denke* for talking."

His eyebrows drew together. "I can't leave you when you're so upset."

She fixed a smile on her face. "I'll be fine."

"You will?"

She nodded.

"Why don't I stop by your place after work?" he asked.

"*Nee,* I'll be okay. I'll go into town and take a walk in the park. That always cheers me up."

"Are you sure?"

"*Jah.* You better go. Your *Mamm* will be waiting." He was just about to say something and then she added, "Go on." She turned away and climbed into the buggy. "I feel better now after our talk."

"Really?"

"*Jah, denke.* Bye, Jeff." She jiggled the reins and Nigel made his way onto the road.

CHAPTER 17

WHEN SHE HAD PARKED the buggy, May got out and walked in the sunshine. She did her best thinking when she was alone and walking. A person came walking toward her — a young woman, she realized. May noticed the woman's gaze was focused on her. May returned the look, wondering if she knew her.

"May?" the young woman asked.

May stared with a curious expression, wondering how this woman knew her.

"It's Jenny," the woman said.

The only Jenny she knew was a girl she'd grown up with, who was two years older than she. "Jenny Miller?"

"Yeah, it's me."

With her mouth open in shock, May stared at Jenny's short cropped hair. That's why she hadn't recognized her — she wore her hair like a boy. Jenny

Miller had left the community some years before. "How are you doing?"

Jenny closed the gap between them and gave May a quick hug. "I'm doing great." She then stepped back and looked her up and down. "You're still in the community I see?"

"I am."

"That's no good. Have you ever thought of leaving?"

May shook her head and then found herself nodding as though her head had a mind of its own. "Not until today."

"There's a large group of us who've left and we've formed this, um ... kind of a support group." She giggled. "It's an unofficial group. We're all about the same age, a little older than you. You know it's a cult, don't you?"

"What is?" She knew what Jenny meant, though. She'd heard people call the Amish a cult before, but she knew it wasn't. Their members were free to leave if they wanted and no one controlled their minds.

"The Amish."

May shook her head. "I'm not sure what you're talking about."

Jenny stood taller pulling her shoulders back. "They tell you what to think and how to feel and how to react about everything. Everyone needs their free will. God gave everyone a mind, but the Amish don't want to know about that."

"I don't know if that's right."

"You don't know — that's right because you've been brainwashed. Once you're out of it you'll become normal."

"Out of the community?" May stared at Jenny wondering if this was her answer. Was there a way to God, and also to inner happiness, outside of the world in which she had been raised?

"You said you thought about it today."

"Jah, because … I just had a huge argument with my *mudder."* May trembled preferring not to think about it.

"What about?"

May shook her head "It's silly, really."

"Tell me."

Anger and dismay washed over her as the despair clouded her mind. "April did something and then all of a sudden everyone's blaming me. It always happens like that because we're twins. I get lumped in together with her. People don't understand we're two different people. We're not just 'the twins.'"

"I can see why that would be hard."

"It is."

"Is it something that will be okay after a time? I mean, did your *mudder* throw you out of your house?"

"Nee, but I'm sick of the way my folks treat me."

"It's all part of it, May. They've been brainwashed too. Listen, if you want to leave I've got a spare bedroom in my apartment and I can get you a job as a waitress."

May's fingertips flew to her mouth. She had often

thought about having a completely different life. This was her chance and it was being offered to her. She didn't have anything to lose because William didn't like her. He'd made that clear. And, her parents would be happy to be left alone, just the two of them, she was certain of that. "It certainly sounds tempting."

"Take the plunge, what do you have to lose? There's a whole world you know nothing about. I can't believe you've never been on *rumspringa*. Every young person's supposed to try the *Englisch* life, otherwise, how can they make an informed choice to join the community?"

"This support group … you made it sound like none of them ever intend on going back."

"Nee, they don't. Others come to us and then return. Becky Fisher was staying in my place for a whole year."

"Oh, I didn't know. She's getting married soon."

"It cleared her mind and then she felt she wanted to go back and she did. Nothing was keeping her here. We don't stop people if they want to live the Amish life."

May sighed. "But if I die when I'm on *rumspringa* I wouldn't be on the narrow path."

"That's just a bunch of lies to keep you doin' what you're doin.'"

"I'm not so sure about that. That's what I believe. I respect that you believe differently. but …"

"What about April?"

May was slightly annoyed. What did April have to do with her? "She's married and she's moved communities."

"Ah, yes, I did hear that."

"Maybe I will try it. I've really got nothing holding me to the community. I mean, what would it hurt? I work a couple of hours a day at the school, but Deborah could easily find someone else. I could try it for a few weeks and see how I like it."

"Excellent. We'll have so much fun."

"How much is the room?"

"Nothing until you start getting paid."

"Really?" With Jenny being so generous it was too good a deal to let pass.

"It's a large place with a bunch of us living there. You might not know them all, but you soon will." She looked her up and down. "You can borrow some of my clothes too. We're about the same size."

"Thanks. That's generous. I never had a job. I've just worked at the school and that doesn't pay."

Jenny burst out laughing. "It doesn't matter. We all help each other. We wouldn't expect any rent until you get a job. And I'll organize that with my boss."

"Truly?"

Jenny nodded.

May took a deep breath, and then blurted out, "Okay, I'll take you up on your offer."

"Excellent. It was fate, me running into you today. How about I get Ralf to collect you this afternoon?"

This all sounded too good to be true; she wouldn't have to put up with her mother's frosty attitude or the angry stares from her father. That always happened every time they disapproved of her. "About what time do you think?"

"He finishes work at five so he could come and get you around six?"

"That would be perfect. I can't believe this is happening. Is it really okay that I stay with you?"

"Yes. Someone just moved out of the spare room in the apartment."

"Great. And you can really get me that job even though I've got no experience?"

"Sure can. I work at a restaurant and they're always needing people to cover more shifts."

"It sounds good to me."

"Well, how are you goin' to do this?" Jenny asked.

"I guess I'll go home and tell my folks." May bit her lip, not looking forward to that part of it.

Jenny laughed. "Don't worry. It's like ripping off a Band-Aid."

"My *mudder* would think I'm running away with a man when she sees a man in the car."

"That's good thinking. I'll come too."

"Okay." May smiled, relieved.

"She might be upset, but tell her you'll visit her. Unless she doesn't want that. Some Amish parents won't talk to their *kinner* until they come back from *rumspringa.* And never, if they don't come back."

"I don't think mine will be like that. I'm sure they'll be glad of the break from me."

"Okay, well … whatever. We'll be there about six-thirty, all right?"

"Yes, but are you sure it'll be okay, me staying with you?"

"It'll be fine. I'll see you tonight." Jenny leaned in and touched May on the forearm giving her a bright smile.

May turned around and headed back to her buggy feeling she had a good reason to be happy. This was her chance at freedom, and her chance to grow up away from her parents and away from the community.

She climbed into the buggy with one regret. With them collecting her in a few hours, it didn't leave her time to talk with Mary. May wanted Mary to know that her leaving had nothing to do with how she felt about April's revelation. She didn't want Mary and Samuel to hate her as well.

WHEN MAY GOT HOME and told her mother the news, her mother was upset.

May explained, "The bishop says people can go on *rumspringa*. It's expected that all young people do."

"I know that, but you and April always said you wouldn't."

May was more than a little annoyed to have April mentioned again when she was talking about herself. "I've changed my mind." She moved forward and put her arm around her mother's shoulder. "I won't be far away."

"First April goes and now you. I only have your *vadder* left and what if something happens to him?" Her mother sobbed.

"It won't. If something does, I'll come back."

It was heart-wrenching for May to think of leaving her mother and father — even though she'd been cross with them and they'd had this falling out.

On the tick of six-thirty a car pulled up in the drive. It was an old blue car and smoke was pouring from the exhaust so badly May hoped the car would make it into town. Thankfully, her father didn't say anything about it. She hugged both her parents goodbye as the two of them stared in shock at Jenny and her short hair. May knew they were hoping she wouldn't cut her hair although neither said anything.

With a bag of clothing tucked under her arm, May got into the backseat with Jenny.

"You made it," Jenny said, as the car chugged back down the driveway.

"I did."

"You remember Ralf, don't you?"

"Yeah, hi, Ralf."

"Hiya." Ralf gave a little wave. May's best recollection of him was that he would be in his mid-twenties now, and he had always been a loner. He'd left the Amish some time ago.

All the way to the apartment, Ralf and Jenny were

talking about the people who lived with them. It seemed Ralf wasn't a loner anymore. He couldn't stop talking. May wasn't used to single men and women who weren't siblings living under the same roof. They told her there were six of them in all and she was to be the seventh. "It must be a large place."

"It is. We're kicking Paul out of the room you're taking over because he's been there six months and hasn't paid rent. He'll have to stay on the couch."

"Oh, I don't want to disturb anyone." She wasn't sure if she remembered a Paul around her age from the community.

Ralf laughed. "Don't worry about him. He loves the couch. He's there all day and half the night playing video games. He's so lazy. He won't have the irritation of having to get up to go sleep in the bedroom. He can just sleep in front of the TV."

"Oh. Doesn't he work?" May asked.

"No."

CHAPTER 18

AFTER A QUICK TOUR of the musty-smelling apartment, May was shown to her room and then left alone to settle in. The rooms were tiny and that explained why there were so many of them. May's was the size of a shoebox and less than half the size of her room at home. There was space enough for only a single bed. Just as well she hadn't brought many belongings with her. She reminded herself to be grateful for the roof over her head. The saving grace was a reasonably spacious built-in wardrobe.

There were no sheets on the mattress and May regretted not thinking about practicalities such as sheets and pillows. She'd always taken those things for granted. At least she'd thought to bring a towel. With her bag still under her arm, she leaned forward to check out the mattress looking for bed bugs or other nasties. Never having seen such things, she wasn't quite sure what they looked like. Even though the mattress was old and stained, there was nothing crawling on it. Then May considered sleeping on the floor figuring it had to be cleaner.

After she had put her clothes in the wardrobe that was still half full of men's clothes, she found Jenny in the kitchen making dinner. "Is there a sheet I can borrow?"

"Sure. You can have a couple of mine, and a blanket."

"Thanks. I didn't think to bring any."

"We're not in Kansas anymore, Dorothy," Paul yelled out from the couch.

"Ignore him," Jenny said. "We all do."

"Shut up!" Paul said with a laugh.

As much as he was outwardly jovial, May was pretty sure Paul resented her for taking his room.

"What's for dinner?" May asked.

"Oh, we all make our own. I forgot to tell you that. I'll share with you until you get on your feet."

"Thanks, Jenny. I'll pay you back."

"No need. We all help each other. You'll find sheets and all that in the cupboard in my bedroom," she repeated. "Help yourself."

"Thanks."

After May made her bed, including a spare pillow from Jenny's cupboard, she came out to the kitchen to talk with Jenny.

"Dinner's cooking," she said. Then she picked up a

pair of gleaming silver scissors and held them in front of her face.

"What are they for?"

"It's hair-cutting time." Jenny looked her up and down. "Change out of those clothes, come on." Jenny headed toward her own room, grabbing May's hand to bring her along. She opened her wardrobe. "Grab what you want. You can't wear those Amish clothes."

"Okay thanks." She picked a dress and Jenny quickly replaced it with jeans and a t-shirt.

"This'll look better."

May nodded.

"Now take off your *kapp.*"

May did as she was told, unpinning her hair and letting it fall down to her waist. "I had to cut it once when it got tangled when I went swimming a few years ago."

Jenny sighed. "You need to cut it to sever ties with the Amish community. It's symbolic."

"I haven't left the Amish for good. I'll most likely go back after a while."

"I know, but when you're out you need to be out properly."

May smoothed down her hair. "I like it the way it is. I like my long hair."

"Just chop about six inches off, and it'll really be fashionable if we cut bangs."

"Do you think so?"

"Yeah." Jenny grabbed May's shoulders and turned

her around to look into the mirror. Then she grabbed her hair and bundled it up showing May how it would look shorter. "See how much better it looks?"

"I don't know."

Jenny slumped onto her bed. "Everyone's like you when they first escape. Too scared to say boo."

"I'm not scared."

"Then show me."

"*Nee.*"

Jenny laughed. "Stop using that talk."

May bit her lip. Jenny had been so good to her, it wouldn't hurt to cut her hair a little. "I'll cut it." She took the scissors from Jenny and cut bangs into her hair. Passing the scissors back to Jenny, she asked, "Can you cut off a few inches at the back?"

A smile spread across Jenny's face.

"I don't want it to be as short as yours."

"I know."

"And don't cut it crooked."

Jenny proceeded to brush out May's hair and then she carefully took off a few inches. Then she feathered out the bangs making them look better. When May looked in the mirror at the finished style, she was pleased with her new look.

"You look awesome," Jenny said. "You'll get a lot of tips if you flirt with the customers."

May opened her mouth, shocked. "I won't."

Jenny laughed. "Lighten up. I was just joking. Come on. Let's eat. Dinner must be ready by now."

May sat down in front of the Spaghetti Bolognese. She mentally said a prayer giving thanks for the food. That was something May would never forget to do.

After dinner, May sat on the couch for a time watching as Jenny joined Paul in playing a video game. Everyone else was out somewhere.

May went to bed early that night to the sounds of people alternately cheering and groaning, depending on whether they were winning or losing their video games. Other people had joined in with watching the game when they'd gotten home from work. Eventually, May managed to push thoughts of bed bugs from her mind, ignore the noise from the living room, and fall sleep.

As she slept, she dreamed about saying goodbye to Nigel — something she'd forgotten to do before leaving home. Then in her dream, her parents sold him and she didn't even know the family who took him. She was crying and begging her father not to sell her beloved horse, but he totally ignored her as though she wasn't even there and he couldn't hear her. It was like she'd died.

Then she ran down the road after Nigel as his new family took him away. Jeff jumped in front of her. He told her to come home; she agreed and followed him until Jenny appeared and said to follow her. As she stood deciding who to follow, Jeff begged her to come with him telling her about a terrible tornado heading their way. He told her she'd die if she went with Jenny.

She was still deciding when she was engulfed in a tornado. It swept her up into the sky before she could stop it. Around and around she was spun until she was spat out high into the sky. As she flew through the air she felt elated, but then her heart lurched as she plummeted toward the earth. She braced herself for the impact ... and then she woke. She sat bolt upright drenched in a cold sweat.

Tears streamed down her face and she knew she'd made the wrong choice by leaving. The dream was symbolic. She wasn't an independent girl like Jenny. She needed her family and her community. They were home, not this place. And, what if her father really had sold Nigel like in her dream? Surely, he wouldn't.

She lay back down, closed her eyes and somehow, she managed to get back to sleep. When she woke again, it was daylight and she felt a little better. Ignoring her dream, she decided she had to give things a go and see what life in the *Englischer* world was really like.

After a quick breakfast, she accompanied Jenny to her job. They arrived at nine o'clock and then they were informed that the usual person filling in as dishwasher was off sick. May was delighted and offered to fill in. Jenny showed her where everything was and told her what to do. May was sure she'd prefer washing dishes to waitressing. That way she wouldn't be on show and she could stay in her own little world away from everyone.

At the end of the day, the boss offered May five shifts a week, five or so hours each. Even though it wasn't a full-time job, May was delighted.

To celebrate, Jenny bought take-out pizza for dinner. Paul, Ralf, and Jenny sat around drinking beer and sharing the pizza. It was all very grown up. May didn't touch the beer because she didn't like the taste of it. And her parents had never drunk beer, so she was wary of alcohol.

CHAPTER 19

AFTER THREE WEEKS at the job that May had thought she'd enjoy, she was sick of it. Those dishes never stopped coming. The heat in the kitchen was unbearable and most of the time she could barely breathe due to lack of ventilation. She longed to be back in the light-filled schoolhouse, and sitting in the sun or the sun-dappled shade while watching the children play during lunch breaks. Doing dishes all day in the heat of the gray kitchen was killing her.

When her shift was over, she walked back toward the apartment wondering how long she'd be there. She wasn't enjoying this lifestyle. Jenny said that was because she never went to the parties and never went out, but she had no interest in doing those things. Jenny and her friends drank and thought that was fun.

All they did at her new home was play video games, watch TV and have friends over to play card games until the early hours of the morning. As she walked, the wind blew her hair across her face annoying her. That wasn't the first time she'd regretted cutting it.

Her mind drifted to how her parents had treated her, and to her argument with April. The whole thing had been April's fault, why couldn't they see that?

She was about to cross the road when she saw a horse and buggy in the distance. With her breath held in her throat, she waited to see if it was someone she knew. When it drew closer, she saw it was Jeff. She couldn't have been more pleased to see him and she stood on the side of the road and waved at him. When he stopped his buggy, she ran over to him. "What are you doing out this way?"

"Looking for you." He gave a crooked smile.

"Looking for me? Is everything all right?"

"*Jah.* I wanted to see how you're doing. Your *Mamm* gave me your address."

"I'm doing okay. You want to come see my apartment?"

"Sure. Jump in and take me to it."

She climbed up next to him, and then figured she didn't really want him to see the dark and depressing place.

"You cut your hair."

She had forgotten about that. "I have."

He didn't make any more comments.

"There's a park down at the end of this road. I'd rather just talk with you there, if that's okay."

Jeff nodded. "Sure, if that's what you want."

"Yeah." Neither of them said a word, and when they arrived at the park, he turned to her. "How are things, really?"

"Fine."

He stared at her and she felt tears stinging in the back of her eyes. Then the tears flooded down her cheeks. She had so much pent-up emotion over everything. She wasn't happy there and neither was she happy at home. Nothing was right. "Why is it that nothing ever works out for me, Jeff?"

He touched her arm. "Please don't cry. Tell me what's wrong."

"Everything. I had a big fight with my *mudder*, that's why I left."

"What was the fight about?"

"It was April's fault. She's the one who told everybody about Lois." She glanced up at him. "I suppose you know about that?"

"Everybody does. Samuel told everybody."

"Oh, that's right."

"If you're not happy in the *Englisch* world, come back to us."

She shook her head. "I haven't really given it much of a chance."

"You look miserable."

"I am a bit miserable. Everything is too fast and I'm living with Jenny and two boys, and other people who come and go. I've lost count. The other night there were two other boys sleeping on the couches."

He didn't say anything, but she could feel his disapproval. "We each have a room, so don't think anything bad. Everyone who lives there does, except Paul, but he doesn't mind."

"I wasn't thinking anything bad."

"No one wants me back in the community."

He turned more to face her directly. "What do *you* want?"

"I can't live here and neither can I go back." She shrugged her shoulders. "I don't belong anywhere."

"If it weren't for the argument with your *mudder*, would you go home?"

"I don't know. I just can't face her or *Dat*."

"In my experience, parents are the most forgiving of creatures."

She glanced at him and gave a little laugh.

He smiled. "It's true."

"I don't know, things were said. They think I'm to blame for everything."

"Things are often said in anger or impatience, but things can be unsaid, or apologies can be made. You know the story of the prodigal son?"

"*Jah.*"

"You can be the prodigal *dochder*."

May laughed again. "I'm not the one who's done wrong. I'm not the one who needs to apologize."

"It doesn't matter, does it? In your eyes you're right,

in your *mudder's* eyes she is. It depends whose eyes you're viewing from."

He wasn't making sense, but he was making her feel better.

"I don't like to see you upset. You were happier in the community, weren't you?"

"Jah."

"Let's go, then. Grab your things and I'll take you home."

In her heart, that's what she wanted to do. "But my job ... and the room here. I need to pay them for the room ... I need to get my pay."

"How much do you owe them for the room?"

"One hundred and twenty so far."

He pulled out a roll of cash and peeled off notes. "There. And here's an extra hundred and twenty to help them find someone else for the room."

She sniffed. "I'll pay you back."

"Don't worry."

"I will."

He shook his head. "We can talk about that later."

"You'll take me home?"

"Jah."

May had never felt so relieved. "Okay, you wait here."

"I'm not going anywhere."

She jumped down from the buggy and jogged back to the flat. When May opened the door, she was pleased the boys and Jenny were at work and Paul was still asleep on the couch. A giggle nearly escaped her lips when she noticed Paul still had a game controller in his hand.

After she packed her things, she wrote a quick note of thanks to Jenny and left that along with the money on her bed.

It was awful to leave the restaurant without giving notice, but she had been hired on a casual basis. Then she looked down at her clothes, and quickly raced back to her room and changed into her Amish clothes. Feeling more normal, she hurried out to Jeff as she stuffed her hair into her Amish *kapp*.

CHAPTER 20

"Denke for this." May climbed into Jeff's buggy feeling like she was making a great escape.

"I've nothing better to do." He turned the buggy around.

Now she saw the mature side of Jeff as well as his sense of practicality. He gave her a big smile as he moved the horse and buggy back up the road.

"What made you come to find me?" May asked.

"I missed you. Things weren't the same without you there and I knew I needed to do something about it."

"You rescued me."

"I had to."

She pushed the bangs back under her *kapp.* "I just wish I hadn't cut my hair."

"It'll grow back. Don't worry about it."

"I guess you're right. It will grow, won't it?"

He chuckled. "That's right. What was your experience like? Good or bad?"

"Mostly bad. I never fitted in. I always felt like a stranger, an outsider. Everyone said I needed to drink, but I didn't want to."

"You don't belong here."

She nodded and then remembered her dream. Jeff had been urging her to go with him before the tornado struck. Could he be meant to be more than just a friend? She looked over at him, tilting her head as she pondered that idea, and then he caught her eye.

"What?" he asked, grinning.

"Denke, for saving me."

"You might've saved *me* by coming back."

She laughed. "How so?"

"I told you things weren't the same."

Now she was a little nervous around him, no longer seeing Jeff as just an annoying person who liked her. He'd shown strength of character, and William had shown how judgmental he was. It was important to her to have a man who was gentle and kind. Maybe that person, the man *Gott* had for her was Jeff? It certainly had seemed that way in her dream and now he'd rescued her for real.

She didn't know if she could ever fall in love with him, but she'd open her mind to love and she was prepared to give it a chance.

"I'm glad you didn't let Jenny lead you astray."

"It was a very different life. And it's not one I

wanted. I was depressed the whole time. You've never left the community, have you?"

"*Nee.* I never wanted to."

"Why not?"

"My *vadder* needs me at the fruit stall."

She laughed thinking it was a typical Jeff answer.

"And there were a few other reasons I guess. I'm happy here and I don't see any reason to leave. I've had friends go and come back and they've told me what it's like out there. It's nice to have the safe protected feeling here in the community where everyone looks after each other. It's a dog-eat-dog world out there, they tell me. No one cares about anyone like they do here in the community."

"Jenny cared about me."

"Sure, you can have friends, but that's different."

When they turned into May's drive she was suddenly nervous. Her heart pounded and she could scarcely breathe. She sent up a quick silent prayer and hoped she'd be welcomed back.

"You want me to come in with you?"

She saw her mother looking out the kitchen window. "I think this is something I have to do alone." She swallowed hard. "I'll be okay. *Denke* for coming to get me, Jeff."

"Stop it. Stop thanking me." He laughed and she leaned forward and gave him a quick little kiss on the cheek. Then she grabbed her things and got out of the buggy. By the time she reached the front door, she heard his buggy moving away.

Her mother opened the door. "You're back."

"Is that okay?"

Mamm nodded, and held out her arms and May stepped in for one of her mother's hugs as tears again rolled down her cheeks.

She recalled what Jeff said about apologies. "I'm sorry I'm such a bad *dochder.*"

"You aren't at all. It was my fault too. Tempers flare and things get said in anger. Things that never should be said. I'm sorry, May."

"Me too," May said between sobs.

"I've never been sorry you were born. It was a horrible thing to say and I've been mad with myself ever since for saying it."

May giggled. "I knew you didn't mean it."

Then *Mamm* stepped back. "Now upstairs with you and clean yourself up. You can come down and help me prepare the dinner."

She nodded, wiped her eyes and then headed up the stairs to her bedroom. When she walked in, her bedroom was just as she'd left it. Then she raced to the window, relieved when she saw Nigel in the paddock. It would've been a nightmare for real if her father had sold him, like in her dream. It was then she was reminded of the horrible time she'd had living in that dark overcrowded apartment with all the noise.

The only thing those people had in common was

that they used to be Amish. She'd spent most of the time in her room or washing up because Jenny was out all the time either working or with her boyfriend. She looked out the window of her very own bedroom across the field and silently thanked God for sending Jeff to bring her home—home where she belonged.

WHEN SHE GOT DOWNSTAIRS to help her mother, she asked, "How's Mary?"

"Things are back to normal. Everyone's forgotten about that."

"Oh, that's good." May knew that was definitely not so. People in their community always remembered things like that. Just because no one said anything didn't mean they didn't remember. "I might stop by her *haus* tomorrow if that's all right."

"*Jah.*"

"And then I might see the bishop about getting baptized soon."

A smile spread across her mother's face. "That would be a good idea. Most people get baptized when they return from their *rumspringa.*"

And that was her mother all over. She always liked everyone in her family to do the same things as everyone else.

"One thing you must do right now is call April."

"Why?"

"She's dreadfully worried about you."

"I didn't tell her what I was doing."

Her mother sighed. "I know, and when I told her, she acted like you were kidnapped. She said you would've definitely told her and I said you decided very fast, almost at the last minute."

"I'll call her now."

"Jah, go on."

May headed to the phone in the barn. April answered immediately and May told her everything that had happened. When she eventually ended the call, she felt things were back to normal between herself and April. May didn't ask April if she was happy to be back with Philip because something told May that her twin would always find something to complain about. That's just how she was.

CHAPTER 21

THE VERY NEXT DAY, May knocked on Samuel and Mary's door. Freda, the housekeeper answered her knock and then showed May into the living room where Mary sat holding her new baby, Sam. Lois, still a little young for school, was playing on the floor.

A smile spread across Mary's face. "May, sit down with me. I heard you've been on *rumspringa.*"

"*Jah,* and now I'm back."

"That was fast."

May giggled. "Well, I suppose it was. It just wasn't right for me. I couldn't wait to come home. I just wanted to let you know that I had nothing to do with your secret being exposed."

"I didn't think you did. Anyway, I think it was a blessing that it came out."

"Why's that? Now Samuel isn't a minister, so that can't be good."

"That doesn't matter. He and I are okay with it."

May knew it did matter. It must have been embarrassing to both of them. "How's Sam?"

Mary looked down lovingly at her new son. "He's fast asleep. He's such a good *bu.*" She looked back at May. "I just don't know how April found out about it. Do you know?"

"It was the midwife. Not Rebecca, the other one you had, Marilyn's cousin. April was good friends with another cousin of hers, and the midwife must've told the story to the cousin April knows. The cousin told April, probably thinking it would never get back to anyone and of course not naming names. I think I've got that right. Anyway, April said she recognized the circumstances and put two and two together, so to speak."

Mary nodded. "I see. Well, that makes sense. I do remember I said I would have you and William over for dinner."

May slowly shook her head. "That's all over with now. He's not for me."

"He's not?"

"Nee. There's someone else I think I might like, but I'm not sure."

"Would you like me to have you and the mystery man over for dinner?"

May burst out laughing. *"Nee,* that's okay. *Denke,* though."

Mary smiled through a yawn.

"Oh, I should go. You're probably tired."

"I am — I didn't get much sleep. Sam was awake most of the night. He thinks night is day and day is night. I'm sorry things didn't work out with you and William."

"It's okay. *Jah,* it'll all be okay. I didn't really know him. I just thought I liked him."

"And you know the mystery man better?"

"*Jah,* I've known him all my life. I grew up with him. He's always been a good friend to me and I know he really likes me it's just that ... oh, I really should go." May jumped to her feet.

"It's okay. You can tell me."

May smoothed down her dress. "Another time. I can see you're tired."

"*Denke,* for stopping by. I'm happy you're back home." Mary pushed herself to her feet.

"Me too."

Mary leaned forward and they hugged each other, careful of the baby in Mary's arms.

May DROVE her buggy away from Mary's house wanting to see Jeff again. She'd seen a different side of him and she wanted to know more.

When she got back home, her mother had a list of things for her to buy from the markets. It wasn't even their regular shopping day, but now she had an excuse to see Jeff and she hoped he'd be there. Jeff's family ran the largest fruit and vegetable stall at the biggest farmers market in town. The family also had a large apple orchard, too, one of the biggest in the region.

On her way to the market, she stopped by the school. She had to give her apologies to Deborah for disappearing so suddenly.

It was lunchtime when she got there, and when she walked into the playground she was swamped with children who wanted to say hello. Deborah saw her and wandered over.

"Hello, Deborah. I came to see you for a couple of minutes if you have the time."

"Of course. Now, children, Miss May and I need to have a quiet moment. She'll say goodbye to you before she leaves." The children went back to playing and left them alone. "Let's go over here into the shade," Deborah suggested.

May didn't think Deborah seemed too upset with her. "I just wanted to see you to say I'm very sorry for leaving with no notice."

"Oh, May, you don't have to apologize. You were doing us all a favor by being here. You don't owe us anything."

"I made a commitment and then I just went off on *rumspringa*." May shook her head. It didn't seem right that Deborah wasn't annoyed with her. If the situation were reversed, she'd be fuming.

"I was young once. I know what it's like. Would you like to return now that you're back? You are staying on?"

"You mean it?"

"I sure do. The children like you and it takes a lot of pressure from me. If you agree to come back, I'll see if the board can raise some extra funds to pay you for at least the equivalent of one full day a week."

May gasped. "That would be a dream come true."

"I can't promise anything, but I can ask."

"It doesn't matter if they don't. I would very much like to help out every day like I was doing."

"Okay." She reached out her hand. "Good to have you back."

She shook Deborah's hand. *"Denke,* Deborah."

"I'm guessing you didn't enjoy your *rumspringa?"*

May shook her head. "I didn't."

"That's the shortest amount of time—"

"I know. I wasn't gone for long, but it felt like ages to me."

Deborah laughed.

"I should say goodbye to the children, and can I tell them I'll be back tomorrow?"

"Sure."

May took a few steps away from Deborah and was engulfed in a sea of questions.

"Are you coming back, Miss?" one boy asked.

"Jah, I'll be back tomorrow."

The children cheered and their smiling faces

165

brightened May's mood even further. May was able to get away from the excited children when Deborah rang the bell signifying their after-lunch playtime was over.

As May climbed up into her buggy, she felt like her life was going somewhere.

CHAPTER 22

WITH HER NEWFOUND interest in Jeff, May walked into the farmers market while saying a little prayer. She didn't want anything to start between them if it was only going to end. It was comforting to know that he liked her, but she couldn't let him know she was interested unless she thought she could fall in love with him for real. What she wanted was those feelings in the tummy that William had given her. Could Jeff, the boy she'd known all her life, ever make her feel that way?

Everything about Jeff made sense. He had a good heart, he was sensible, and he was a hard worker. She saw him from a distance and when she got closer, she saw he was talking to a young woman from their community. It was Michelle Grovner. When they shared a laugh, May looked on in horror. She must've stopped still because someone ran into her. "Oh, I'm so sorry," she said to the man who'd run into her.

"Sorry," he mumbled as he sidestepped and hurried past.

May stood there looking back at Jeff and Michelle. Michelle was flirting with him. May could tell from the way she was looking at him all coy-like and twirling her *kapp* strings about her fingers. May got feelings in her stomach all right, but they weren't butterflies. It was the churning gut-wrenching knowledge that she'd left things too late.

Then, a thought came to her. What would April do? April would walk over there and break up their conversation, and it might be a good thing to do that, but she couldn't. Her mother's list fell from her hand as she walked out of the farmers market.

When she was halfway to the buggy, she heard rushing footsteps behind her and she moved to one side. She'd caused one collision today and didn't want another.

Jeff jumped in front of her. "Is this yours?"

She inhaled sharply and then looked at the list. *"Jah.* It is mine." She took it from him. *"Denke.* I didn't realize … I must've dropped it."

He placed his hands on his hips. "Where are you rushing off to?"

"Oh, well, I don't know."

He laughed. "Why not?"

Looking down at the paper she'd crumpled in her hand, she murmured, "I was going shopping."

"So, why were you leaving? I don't see evidence that you've done any shopping."

"I'm just starting out."

He chuckled. "Shops are this way."

She nodded and straightened out her crumpled list.

"What's up with you, May? Are you ill?"

She stared at his concerned face. "I'm fine."

"I've got to get back to work. Do you need any fruit or vegetables?"

"I do."

"Come on. I'll select them for you." He started walking and her feet were firmly planted on the ground.

"Is that what you were doing for Michelle?"

He turned back and the smile left his face. "Wait a minute. Michelle and I are just friends."

"Hmm. That's what they all say."

He narrowed his eyes. "Are you worried about Michelle? Do you think I like her?"

She didn't like to admit her interest in him at this point, but she had to know. "Are you?"

"*Nee.*"

"Are you sure because you looked pretty friendly over there?"

He took a step toward her. "May, are you jealous?"

She looked away from him. "Don't be silly."

"It seems that's the only explanation for you saying these things."

"I'm not."

"Good because there's no reason for you to be worried about Michelle or any other girl. I'm waiting for you."

"Waiting?"

"I like you. It's as plain and simple as that. I know I'm not much to look at. I'm not handsome or anything …"

"I wouldn't say that."

He chuckled. "I'm hoping what's inside me, at some stage of my life, will make up for the rough packaging *Gott* placed me in."

She giggled. "I've never heard anyone say anything quite like that."

"Anyway, let's get you fixed up with some vegetables before my *vadder* comes looking for me."

She walked alongside of him. "I wouldn't want you to get into trouble."

He stopped suddenly and faced her. "May, would you come on a picnic with me on Saturday?"

Her head spun. Things were moving quickly. "Err… I don't know."

"Give me an answer. I won't be upset if you say no. Okay, I will be upset, but I won't show it."

She laughed. "What kind of a picnic?"

"Leave that up to me. I'll collect you at ten." He didn't wait for an answer, and she went along with his decision. Now she was going on her first official date with Jeff.

He selected the best fruits and vegetables for her,

and gave her a few extra items that weren't on her list and then helped her carry it out to the buggy.

"*Denke,* Jeff. You better go back. Your *vadder* will wonder why you're paying me such special attention."

"Okay, I'll go back." He put the last box in the buggy for her. "Don't forget Saturday."

"I won't forget." She got into the buggy and drove away from the parking lot. When she looked in her rear-view mirror, she saw Jeff at the entrance of the markets, staring at her. She couldn't help but smile. Now she was flattered to know he felt that way about her. It had taken thinking she'd lost him to another woman to make her see how much she wanted him.

SATURDAY FINALLY ARRIVED and May was on that picnic with Jeff. She'd no longer thought about William every waking moment. Her thoughts were now of Jeff.

In the middle of eating chicken sandwiches on a checkered blanket, Jeff threw out an impulsive question. "Marry me, May?"

May giggled. "*Nee,* I can't. What would people say?"

"Congratulations. You got a good man there, May."

May playfully slapped him on his arm. "You know what I mean. We've only gone out once and that's only today. No one knows that we ..."

"Stop worrying what others think. If you want to marry me say yes, if you don't, then say no. It's as simple as that. Mind you, I'll be crushed if you refuse me."

"You just said not to worry about others." It was surprising to her that she was having such a good time with him. It was as though they belonged together.

He laughed. "I wasn't talking about me."

"It's too soon for me. I want to be sure."

"Okay. I can respect that. I don't mind waiting until you're sure."

He passed her another chicken sandwich. When she took it from him, she said, "Thank your *mudder* for these sandwiches."

"I made them," he said looking offended, which made her giggle.

"Ah, you're joking with me now?"

"Just a little."

They sat, talking and eating for what seemed like a couple of hours, but in no time, it got dark. "Oh, it's late. I better get you home."

"They'll be wondering where I am."

"They won't be worried. They know you're with me."

On the way home, May once again recalled that dream where Jeff was calling her to go with him. Now she knew more fully what that dream meant. She belonged in the Amish community and she belonged with Jeff, but she wasn't going to agree to marry him just yet.

When he stopped the buggy outside her front door,

she turned to him. *"Denke* for a lovely day. I hope *Mamm* hasn't been worried with me being home so late."

"I told you she knows you're with me. She'll be fine. Do you want me to talk with her?"

"Nee, it's fine."

May jumped down from the buggy. "Bye, Jeff."

"I'll see you soon, May." He turned his buggy around and May watched as he headed down the road.

Behind her, she heard the door open and turned to see her father. "Where have you been?"

"Out with Jeff." She could see her father wasn't pleased. *"Mamm* knew where I was." She walked past her father and headed to the kitchen where she found her mother crying at the table. "What's wrong, *Mamm?"* She rushed to her side.

"It's April. She's on her way back here. She says she doesn't want to live with Philip anymore."

"Oh, that's dreadful."

Her mother stopped crying for a moment and stared at her. "I'll have no *grosskinner.* Not if you don't get married."

"I'm working on it, *Mamm.* Believe me." May pulled out a chair and sat next to her mother, and put her head on her shoulder.

"April has no shame coming back here to be a burden on our family."

"I'm sure she'll find work."

"Nee, I don't mean that. She'll ruin our good name."

May sat up straight and licked her lips. "I'm sure she just needs a few weeks away. She went back before she was ready."

"Do you think that's all?"

"*Jah*, I do. Unless …"

"Unless what?"

"Is there a reason she's not happy with Philip?"

"I don't know." Her mother sobbed into her handkerchief and May's father came into the room and sat down with them.

May's father cleared his throat. "You'll have to talk sense into April. She doesn't listen to anyone else."

"She's never listened to me." May shook her head trying to think if there was ever a time April had taken any notice of anything she said. She couldn't think of one time. "When will she be here?"

"Tomorrow."

"Okay. I'll try to talk with her, but I think it's best everyone leaves her alone to sort herself out. If no one says anything to her it'll be much better."

Dat shook his head. "*Nee.* We can't make things comfortable here for her. She belongs with her husband."

"That's right," *Mamm* agreed.

May sighed. All she wanted to do was think about Jeff and decide whether she'd marry him. Trust April to come back and ruin everything—again.

. . .

THAT NIGHT, May went to sleep thinking about Jeff. She'd had the best day of her life with him. They'd laughed and they'd talked. The only problem she had was that she had thought she'd marry a different kind of man, someone older and someone who looked a certain way. One thing in Jeff's favor was that those butterflies had taken up residence in her tummy now, so maybe he was her man.

CHAPTER 23

Rebecca woke up after Jacob had left for work. When she reached for her robe, she heard babbling coming from Micah's room. It was the first night that Micah had slept in that room since they'd been living there. Anne always had him over at her place. She walked into his room to see his smiling face. *"Gut Mayrie,* Micah." She reached out and picked him up. "Let's get some food for you."

Just as they reached the kitchen she saw a buggy leaving. Leaning forward at the window, she saw Anne was heading somewhere. Everything was working out perfectly. Anne had somewhere to be and Micah was under her roof, so she could be a proper mother to him.

Before she was done feeding Micah, she heard the rumbling of buggy wheels and the clip-clops of a horse's hooves. "Hmm. She didn't stay away long." She half stood up and saw it was May and not Anne. "Oh, she's an early visitor."

When May knocked on the door, Rebecca called out for her to come in.

A flustered-looking May walked into the kitchen and sat down. "Hello, Micah. Oh, look at him eating."

"You look worried," Rebecca said.

"I am. So much has happened. I don't know where to start."

"You could start by putting the kettle on for me while I finish with Micah."

"Sure." May jumped up, filled the teakettle and popped it on the stove. "There. That's all done." She sat back down.

"What's happening?"

"April's coming back. She doesn't want to live with her husband anymore. I'm supposed to change her mind. I mean, how am I going to do that?"

Rebecca shook her head and then spooned another portion of cereal into Micah's mouth. "I don't know. She's pretty determined."

"I said, just leave her be, and *Dat* said he didn't want to make things too comfortable for her."

"You're in a difficult situation."

"The other thing is that Jeff wants to marry me."

"What?" Rebecca shrieked.

"Jeff wants to marry me."

"I heard what you said. I'm so happy for you." Rebecca jumped up, leaned over and hugged May.

"I haven't said yes."

"Oh." Rebecca sat back down. "I've always liked Jeff."

"Me too, as a friend."

"Nothing more?" She could see the agony on May's face. She'd had that same feeling when she knew Jacob liked her and she was uncertain.

"We had a picnic yesterday and everything went so well and he ruined it by asking me to marry him."

Rebecca giggled. "That's so funny."

"Everything is happening so fast. How can I think straight when April is here? She'll ruin things with Jeff and me. She always ruins things and causes trouble along the way."

Rebecca knew that was true, having experienced April's troublemaking first-hand. "All I can tell you is that when you know someone's the right one, you'll be all right."

"I'd always pictured myself with someone different from Jeff."

"Me too. I mean, I never saw myself married to someone older, and with a child, a man whose *fraa* had just gone home to *Gott*. Sometimes in life we have to go with the heart and leave our expectations behind."

"I do like Jeff and I think I could love him in time. My feelings for him are growing."

"Good. Don't overthink things."

May nodded. "I won't. I'll try not to. What am I going to do about April?"

Rebecca tried to spoon another mouthful of food

into Micah's mouth, but he kept moving his head. She left it a moment. "I'm not sure. Why are you so worried?"

"My life's just going good. I've got a couple of hours at the school each day, and now things are going well with Jeff. For the first time, things seem to be going my way. I just know in my heart that April will spoil things." The kettle whistled and May jumped up to make the tea.

"I don't see how April can change things for you. Won't she be too wrapped up with herself and her marital problems?"

May sat down as she placed the pot of tea on the table. "I hope so."

MAY SHARED the pot of tea with Rebecca, and then she went home — arriving just as April was pulling up in the taxi.

Her father had taken the day off work to talk some sense into April and have her agree to return to her husband.

April didn't get a welcome greeting from anyone and then their father ordered everyone into the living room. It was time for one of his serious talks.

When April sat, she looked around at everyone. "Why are you all acting so hostile?"

"Because you've left your husband again," their mother said.

"I fooled you all, hahaha!" April cackled with her hands over her face.

Their father frowned at her. "What did you fool us about?"

"I'm expecting! Surprise."

Everyone was stunned, and *Mamm* was the first to speak. "You're not leaving Philip?"

"Nee, Mamm. I'm expecting … a *boppli."*

Mamm looked at *Dat,* who grinned and *Mamm* jumped up and hugged April. May ran to her as well and both of them hugged April. *Dat* stepped in and wrapped his arms around his girls for a group hug.

When everyone stepped back, April sat back down. "You should've seen your faces."

"When is your due date?" *Mamm* asked.

"Five months' time."

"And you didn't know when you were here before?" May asked.

"I suspected."

May stared at her twin wondering how she could keep such a secret from her. "I'm going to be an aunty."

"Is Philip excited?" *Mamm* asked.

"Jah, he's hoping for twins."

"Nee, not twins." May giggled.

"Twice the trouble." *Dat* shook his head and everyone laughed.

Mamm put her arm around April. "I can't believe you made us think you were leaving Philip."

"Jah, I had you all worried for nothing."

May frowned at her twin for thinking it was funny to worry her family, but now she was relieved. This was the best news she could think of. She would soon have a niece or nephew to fuss over.

That night, April confided in May how much she'd changed since marrying Philip. She certainly seemed more content now that she was having a *boppli.* May in turn, told her twin about her feelings for Jeff. She thought April would laugh or say something negative. Instead, she was encouraging.

"I think you should marry him," April said.

May bit her lip. "Maybe."

"What better man is there around for you?"

May didn't see that as a good enough reason to marry him. "It wasn't long ago that I liked someone else."

"Jah, but you didn't know William, not properly."

May nodded. "That's true. I could've done something about that. I never really even talked to him because I'm too shy."

"There's still time. William's not dating anyone, is he?"

"Nee, but I'm convinced Deborah likes him. She's always running over to talk to him when school finishes."

"When do you see Jeff next?"

"I don't know."

April gasped. "He didn't make another time to see you?"

"Nee. Is that bad?"

April looked away.

May pulled on her arm. "Is it? You must tell me."

When April stared back at her, she said, "I'm just thinking …"

"What?"

"What if he's going around asking girls to marry him and he'll marry the first one who says yes?"

May leaned back onto her elbows and looked up at the ceiling. She remembered him talking to that other girl at the markets. They certainly had looked friendly. *"Nee,* he wouldn't do that."

"Okay."

"Do you think he would?" May stared at April for an answer.

"How would I know? You know him better than I do."

"Nee he wouldn't."

THAT NIGHT, thanks to April putting doubts in May's mind, May was unable to sleep. She'd had a lovely time with Jeff, but she couldn't shake off the picture of him talking to that girl at the markets. What if he'd asked her to marry him too?

AT SCHOOL THE NEXT DAY, Deborah wasn't feeling well,

so May encouraged her to go home. She never expected what would happen next. After school, she was outside waiting for the children to leave when William walked over to her.

"May, can we talk?"

"Sure." She looked past him and saw his girls waiting in the buggy.

"Mary told me how I made you feel when I talked to you about what happened with Lois. I realize now you had no part in it. So, I'm sorry."

She was pleased he was apologizing to her now, but she'd told him at the time she had nothing to do with it. Why did he believe Mary and not her?

"Will you forgive me?"

"Of course. *Jah.*"

He gave an embarrassed chuckle. "Can I make it up to you by having you over for dinner one night soon? The girls love it when we have guests. We haven't done that for some time."

May knew that meant they hadn't had Deborah as a guest for dinner. This was what she'd been waiting for, but now she wasn't thrilled like she thought she would've been. Now she knew for certain how much she liked Jeff. *"Denke,* but it's not necessary."

"Please, it would make the girls happy."

"I have to give *Mamm* help around the place."

He slowly nodded. "Okay. If you ever change your mind let me know." He turned and walked away.

No longer did she find him as attractive as she once

had. What's more, she was longing to see Jeff's smiling face.

When all the children had left, she locked up the school and headed to the markets. When she saw Jeff she was going to use the excuse of picking up extra vegetables. April would be cross with her because she wanted to spend time with her before she went back home, but she needed to see Jeff.

CHAPTER 24

MAY WAS ONLY HALFWAY to the markets when Jeff's buggy came toward her. She waved to him and he pulled his buggy off to the side of the road.

She too pulled her horse over and then Jeff hurried across the road to meet her. "Where are you off to?"

"I was going to the markets. Where are you going?"

He chuckled. "To see you. I was trying to get to the school before you left, but time got away from me."

"You were coming to see me?"

"*Jah.*" Cars swooshed past them. They were in one of the main streets at a busy time of the day. "Can we go somewhere quieter to talk? That is, if you're not in a rush?"

"Sure. I'm not in a hurry. We can go somewhere in my buggy and leave yours here if you want?"

"Okay."

He got into May's buggy and she turned the first

corner and they parked the buggy down a side road. "I really can't leave my horse there too long. I just wanted to tell you ... I was coming to see you ..." He breathed out heavily. "It's hard to say."

She held her breath. Was he going to tell her he was dating Michelle or, even worse, marrying her? "Just say it. I can take it."

He chuckled and then swallowed hard. "I don't want to push you away."

Then she knew he still liked her and still wanted to marry her. "What is it? It must be important for you to be coming to see me." She figured she'd help him out. "I was coming to the markets to see you."

"Why?"

"Because I wanted to."

A smile spread across his face. "You wanted to see me?"

"*Jah*, I did."

"Then you must like me a little bit."

She slowly nodded. "I do. If I didn't I wouldn't have gone on that picnic with you."

"I'm happy to hear it."

"I've made up my mind," May said.

"About what?"

"I will marry you, Jeff Whiley."

He chuckled. "You will?"

"*Jah.*" She knew they would be good together. Just because he came in a plain package didn't mean he was that way inside. She'd never known a nicer man or one who'd stood up for her and helped her the way he had.

He took hold of her hand, raised it to his lips and kissed it. *"Denke,* May. I will make you the happiest woman in the world. One day we'll have our own *haus* and our own orchard. I've been saving."

"None of that matters, Jeff. All those things are temporary. As long as we can be together that's all I'll ever need."

"We should tell our folks."

"Can we wait a couple of days? April's just come back and announced she's expecting, so I don't want to take the attention away from her news. She'll be gone soon."

"You're so sweet and caring of others, May. You've got such a good heart."

She giggled. "You see the best in me."

"When I look at you, there is only goodness to see."

She stared into his eyes and then he slowly leaned over and their lips touched. She felt tingles rush through her body and all she wanted was to be in his arms.

"When can I see you again?" he asked.

"Um, tomorrow? Shall I come mid-afternoon to the markets? I'll come as soon as I'm done with school. Unless Deborah is sick again and I'll have to stay all day like I did today."

"I mean see you properly?"

"I don't know. Can I tell you tomorrow?"

"That's good enough for me. Now, I must get my horse and buggy. I can't leave them there like that."

May turned the buggy around and took Jeff back to his horse and buggy. Before he jumped out, he looked her in the eyes. "Don't you change your mind."

She laughed. "I'd never do that."

"Good." He gave her hand another squeeze, and then got out of the buggy.

MAY DROVE BACK HOME as pleased as she could be. She wondered when they'd marry and where they'd live. Jeff's family had a large home, so maybe they'd live there for a while until they got something of their own.

THAT NIGHT, as May listened to April talk about the plans she and Philip had for the baby, she could barely keep in her own news. Then she knew she'd have to have the wedding in the next few months because they couldn't have it when April was due or during the first few months after. It was better to have it while April could travel.

"What's up with you? Aren't you excited?" April asked her.

"I'm thrilled about your news. I can't wait to be an aunt. I just wish you lived closer."

"Me too, but I don't. You'll have to visit me. I won't be able to visit you anymore. Not for a while."

May nodded and held her tongue. Then she knew she wanted April to hear the news at the same time as her folks. The idea came to her that she'd invite Jeff to dinner the following night and once they'd told April and her parents, they could then drive over and tell Jeff's. It would take attention away from April, but then they could share each other's good news and April could plan to come home for the wedding.

THAT NIGHT, April and May slept in the same bed as they had sometimes done when they were younger. They talked all night and May found it hard to keep her good news quiet.

In the morning, April was still asleep when May crept to the barn, rang Jeff and invited him for dinner that night. Thankfully, she'd managed to catch him early before he'd started his long day. He also had been the one to answer the phone that was in the shanty outside his family's house.

When she went back inside, she heard her mother and father talking in the kitchen.

"You're awake early, May," her mother said when she walked in.

"I know. I forgot to let you know I invited Jeff Whiley for dinner tonight."

"Okay." Her mother looked at her father.

"That's good," her father commented. "Is there any reason in particular?"

"You'll find out tonight." She turned to walk out of the kitchen but her mother beat her to the doorway.

"Why's he coming?"

"I thought it was a good idea."

"Who's coming?" April appeared at the doorway.

May looked up to see April finally awake. "I thought you'd be asleep."

"I must be sleep-walking, then. Who's coming?"

"Jeff Whiley. Your *schweschder* invited him tonight for the evening meal," *Mamm* told April.

April walked closer to May. "Is that so?"

"*Jah.*"

"Why didn't you tell me?"

May shook her head. "I forgot about it until now."

"You're lying."

"Girls, please don't start quarreling so early in the day. At least wait until I'm at work."

"You'll all have to wait," May said, wishing her family wasn't so difficult.

"Are you marrying him?" April asked.

May frowned at April, not wanting to let her secret out until Jeff was there by her side. "Don't be silly."

"He is a good match for you," *Mamm* said. "I always thought that."

April stared at their mother. "Since when?"

"Always."

Dat stood. "Time for me to leave."

"Look what you girls have done now. You're making your *vadder* leave early."

"Not my fault," April said. "It's May's."

After their father left for work April and May sat down to eat the scrambled eggs that their mother cooked for them.

April wouldn't let the matter go. "Why's he coming for dinner?"

"Just because I like him and I wanted him to come and see what a loving family I have."

April scoffed. "Yeah, sure."

Now she wanted to tell April and her mother, but she had to wait for Jeff to be there. He was just as excited, as she was that they were announcing their marriage to everyone tonight. They'd barely had time to plan anything, but that made it all the more exciting.

THAT EVENING, May hurried out to meet Jeff when he arrived at the house. She could see from his smiling face he was just as happy as she.

"Have you told anyone?" Jeff asked.

"Nee. But it was hard to keep the news in. I think they suspect, but nothing's been said.

He chuckled, and then got down from his buggy.

"Have you told anyone?" May asked.

He shook his head. "I am sticking to our plan. We tell your folks first. Then, tonight, we go to tell mine. After we finish dinner here."

Side-by-side they walked into the house. When they walked in, they were faced with May's parents and April lined up standing in a row.

"You're getting married?" *Dat* asked.

"*Jah*, how did you know?" Jeff asked.

"A good guess," he said smiling. Then her father stepped forward and shook Jeff's hand. "I'm happy to call you my son-in-law."

"*Denke.*"

Mamm and April gave Jeff a hug, and then May said, "Where's my hug?" They laughed and embraced her. "We had it all planned out. We were going to tell you over dinner."

April shook her head. "You made it too obvious since *Dat* even figured it out."

Mamm said, "We're all delighted. Now let's eat and we can talk about the wedding."

Over dinner, a tentative date was selected. A date that April would be able to make without it being too close to the birth of her first child.

"This is a time for celebrations. First April's news and then yours, May."

May giggled. "I know. Everything happens at once."

"Will your parents be this happy, Jeff?" April asked.

May glared at April for saying such a thing.

"They'll be delighted. Of course they will."

"Hmm. I hope so," April said staring at May.

May decided not to stay for dessert, instead she suggested to Jeff that they go to his place immediately.

She wasn't sure what April would say next, and she didn't want her exciting news to be surrounded in anything but joy.

As they traveled to Jeff's house, May said, "I hope you don't mind we didn't stay too long there."

"*Nee.* Whatever you decide is okay with me. I can't wait to see the happiness on my parents' faces when we tell them the news. I told them you were stopping by."

"Do you think they suspect, too?"

He laughed. "I think so."

"Can you pull over a moment?"

Jeff glanced over at her. "Sure."

May put a hand to her forehead. She'd come over dizzy. "I think I've had too much excitement."

"Are you okay?" He rested a hand lightly on her shoulder.

With him she felt so safe and protected and she knew he'd never change. "I'm good. I just need a moment. Things are happening fast."

"Too fast?"

"*Nee.*"

"If you want to delay things, just say so. I won't mind."

She faced him. "I can't wait to be married to you, Jeff Whiley." She moved closer to him and placed her head on his shoulder.

He rested his head on hers. "We've got a lot to figure out in the next little while. Where we'll live and such."

"I'll leave that up to you. I don't mind where we live."

"Me either."

May closed her eyes and in that moment, she was more content than she'd ever been. This was the beginning of her new life, and he'd brought her back from *rumspringa*. She remembered her dream. The tornado was the life of turmoil she would've had if she didn't have Jeff in her life. Now, she was following him into a life of faith and, with *Gott* by their side, May knew their life and their love would prosper.

After a few more moments, May said, "Okay. Are you ready to go and tell your parents?"

"Mmm, maybe just another minute. It's so noisy there. I like it quiet like it is here with just you." He gently kissed the top of her head.

May closed her eyes again, enjoying the quiet moment with her future husband. She couldn't imagine anyone better than Jeff, her rescuer and her hero. May silently sent up a prayer of thanks, knowing her future with Jeff would be secure because his love covered her completely like a warm blanket. She'd never felt so protected, loved, and safe.

AMISH WOMEN OF PLEASANT
VALLEY

Book 1 The Amish Woman and Her Last Hope

Book 2 The Amish Woman and Her Secret Baby

Book 3 The Amish Widower's Promise

Book 4 The Amish Visitors

Book 5 The Amish Dreamer

Book 6 The Amish School Teacher

Book 7 Amish Baby Blessing

Book 8 Amish Christmas Wedding

Amish Women of Pleasant Valley Boxed Set Books
1 - 4
Amish Women of Pleasant Valley Boxed Set Books
5 - 8

ABOUT SAMANTHA PRICE

USA Today Bestselling author, Samantha Price, wrote stories from a young age, but it wasn't until later in life that she took up writing full time. Formally an artist, she exchanged her paintbrush for the computer and, many best-selling book series later, has never looked back.

Samantha is happiest on her computer lost in the world of her characters. She is best known for the Ettie Smith Amish Mysteries series and the Expectant Amish Widows series.

www.SamanthaPriceAuthor.com

Samantha loves to hear from her readers. Connect with her at:

samantha@samanthapriceauthor.com
www.facebook.com/SamanthaPriceAuthor
Follow Samantha Price on BookBub
Twitter @ AmishRomance
Instagram - SamanthaPriceAuthor

Made in the USA
Monee, IL
30 May 2021